Jane peered no
answer. She ill
there was n

At first, all she saw were the half-filled bottles of wine she and Beau and Buddy had tasted. Then, when she turned her head, she saw that the lid to the stainless steel vat where the wine was being processed was open. That was when she saw the corpse, floating faceup, arms spread . . .

"Someone must have killed him, Hill." Jane's voice was shrill . . .

Hillary sucked in her breath. "Oh my, you don't suppose whoever did it is still . . . " She glanced over her shoulder and grabbed Jane's hand. "Let's get out of here," she said in a hoarse whisper.

Just as she spoke, Jane heard a strange creaking sound and then a thud.

Hillary grabbed her around the waist. "What was that?"

MORE MYSTERIES FROM THE
BERKLEY PUBLISHING GROUP . . .

DOAN AND BINKY MYSTERIES: San Francisco's dazzling detective team is back and better than ever. These detectives have a fashion sense to *die* for . . . "An entertaining cozy with a nineties difference."—*MLB News*

by Orland Outland
DEATH WORE A SMART LITTLE OUTFIT   DEATH WORE A FABULOUS NEW FRAGRANCE
WORE THE EMPEROR'S NEW CLOTHES

DOG LOVERS' MYSTERIES STARRING JACKIE WALSH: She's starting a new life with her son and an ex-police dog named Jake . . . teaching film classes and solving crimes!

by Melissa Cleary
A TAIL OF TWO MURDERS   DEAD AND BURIED
DOG COLLAR CRIME   THE MALTESE PUPPY
HOUNDED TO DEATH   MURDER MOST BEASTLY
FIRST PEDIGREE MURDER   OLD DOGS
SKULL AND DOG BONES   AND YOUR LITTLE DOG, TOO
IN THE DOGHOUSE

CHARLOTTE GRAHAM MYSTERIES: She's an actress with a flair for dramatics—and an eye for detection. "You'll get hooked on Charlotte Graham!"—*Rave Reviews*

by Stefanie Matteson
MURDER AT THE SPA   MURDER AT THE FALLS
MURDER AT TEATIME   MURDER ON HIGH
MURDER ON THE CLIFF   MURDER AMONG THE ANGELS
MURDER ON THE SILK ROAD   MURDER UNDER THE PALMS

PEACHES DANN MYSTERIES: Peaches has never had a very good memory. But she's learned to cope with it over the years . . . Fortunately, though, when it comes to murder, this absentminded amateur sleuth doesn't forgive and forget!

by Elizabeth Daniels Squire
WHO KILLED WHAT'S-HER-NAME?   WHOSE DEATH IS IT, ANYWAY?
MEMORY CAN BE MURDER   IS THERE A DEAD MAN IN THE HOUSE?
REMEMBER THE ALIBI   WHERE THERE'S A WILL
FORGET ABOUT MURDER

HEMLOCK FALLS MYSTERIES: The Quilliam sisters combine their culinary and business skills to run an inn in upstate New York. But when it comes to murder, their talent for detection takes over . . .

by Claudia Bishop
A TASTE FOR MURDER   MURDER WELL-DONE
A PINCH OF POISON   DEATH DINES OUT
A DASH OF DEATH   A TOUCH OF THE GRAPE
A STEAK IN MURDER   MARINADE FOR MURDER

RED WINE GOES WITH MURDER

PAULA CARTER

BERKLEY PRIME CRIME, NEW YORK

RED WINE GOES WITH MURDER

A Berkley Prime Crime Book / published by arrangement with the author

PRINTING HISTORY
Berkley Prime Crime edition / July 2000

The Penguin Putnam Inc. World Wide Web site address is
http://www.penguinputnam.com

ISBN: 0-425-17552-9

Berkley Prime Crime Books are published
by The Berkley Publishing Group,
a division of Penguin Putnam Inc.,
375 Hudson Street, New York, New York 10014.
The name BERKLEY PRIME CRIME and the BERKLEY PRIME CRIME
design are trademarks belonging to Penguin Putnam Inc.

PRINTED IN THE UNITED STATES OF AMERICA

10 9 8 7 6 5 4 3 2 1

RED WINE
GOES WITH
MURDER

1

Jane Ferguson and Hillary Scarborough found the corpse on a warm evening in August. It was in a vat of Côtes du Rhône, full-bodied and robust. The wine that is, not the corpse. Both Jane and Hillary agreed that it just about ruined their vacation.

Jane never dreamed that she would ever make it to France, given the reduced circumstances under which she had been forced to live since Jim Ed had divorced her and married a former Miss Alabama. It was all she could do to make a house payment and buy food for herself and her ten-year-old daughter, Sarah, until she landed a job working for Hillary, whom she thought of as the Martha Stewart of the South—a domestic goddess who ran a catering business and an interior design business under the corporate name of Élégance du Sud. Hillary even had her own local television show in Prosper, Alabama.

Hillary paid Jane a decent salary, albeit not enough for vacations in Europe. Jane found herself there only because Hillary wanted to attend a cooking school in the small Provençal town of Lenoir.

Hillary had planned the trip for months, and it was only in the last two months that she had decided to invite others from her hometown of Prosper to accompany them. That came about after Hillary read of a lovely old seventeenth-century country home for rent. Unfortunately, the rental fee was high enough to give pause even to Hillary, whose financial circumstances were more than comfortable.

"Listen to this," Hillary had said, reading to Jane from the brochure she'd sent for. " 'The house was built in 1636 by the Compte de Lenoir. It was built on the site of the original twelfth-century house built by the compte's ancestor, Jacques de Lenoir, a Knight Templar, after his order was forced out of Jerusalem by the Muslims. A wall of the original twelfth-century house has been incorporated into the present dwelling.' "

"I never knew you were interested in history," Jane had remarked.

Hillary had waved a perfectly manicured, rose-tipped hand at Jane and had gone on reading. " 'The compte built the house to bring his bride, the lovely Jeanne de Sorell, to the region to escape the cold winters of Paris. There are fourteen fireplaces, including the massive stone one in the main hall. The high, arched windows are hung with rich velvet similar to the original window hangings, and the stone floors are covered with duplicates of the Persian carpets the compte bought for his bride.' "

Hillary had stopped reading long enough to glance up at Jane. "Oh, my word, Jane, just think of it. Persian carpets!" She had gone back to her reading, her voice growing high-pitched with excitement. " 'Intricate carvings, unusual for a country house, grace the ceilings, and the furnishings have been carefully selected to recreate a seventeenth-century setting.' "

Hillary had put the brochure down and raised her eyes to heaven. "I have to stay in that house! I just have to!" Hillary always spoke in a breathy Southern accent that made Jane, who was California born and bred, think of hooped skirts and white-columned mansions.

"We could be perfectly happy in the apartments provided by the school." Jane was looking at the enormous rental fee.

Hillary wasn't listening. Instead, she studied the color photos on the brochure. "You know, I think the current proprietor should be told that those carpets would really show to a better advantage if there wasn't so much red in the upholstery."

"You're right, Hill, we can't possibly stay in a place that has too much red in the upholstery."

"Are you trying to talk me out of this, Jane?"

"You're not expecting me to split the rent with you, are you? It's twice my monthly salary."

"Of course not, lamb, but there's some way I can do this. I just know there is. And besides, I might be able to give the proprietor some decorating hints."

"You don't redecorate an authentically restored dwelling, Hillary."

"Nonsense, Jane, everyone can benefit from a few decorating tips."

Jane sighed. "Of course. I forgot for a moment there who I was talking to."

"I don't understand your sarcasm, Jane."

"Sarcasm? *Moi?*"

Hillary waved her hand again, as if to dismiss the topic. "I know, it's a Yankee thing, all that sarcasm. That's why I don't understand it."

Jane could never understand why Hillary thought someone from California was a Yankee, but she didn't have time to ponder it. Hillary was still talking.

"Never mind that. I have to get my thinking cap on and find a way to stay in that house."

"Remember," Jane cautioned, "you promised me I could bring Sarah along. It's summer, and she's not in school, and she wants to bring her best friend along, too. So don't make it too expensive."

Hillary appeared distracted. "I know, I know. Just don't worry about it, Jane. Billy will help me come up with something, and he'll make it a tax write-off, too."

Billy was Hillary's husband, a successful businessman in Prosper who spent his time chasing deals, hunting ducks, and catching bass. Jane had yet to meet him. He seemed always to have just left or to have canceled the engagement each time she was supposed to meet him. He was scheduled to go with them on the trip to France, however.

Within a week, Hillary had called her, excited to tell her the plan. Since the house was large, with several bedrooms, she would advertise in the *Prosper Picyune* as well as on her weekly television show for townspeople who might be interested and could share the rent. She figured that at least four more of Prosper's fifty thousand inhabitants would sign up. As an added incentive, she would act as tour guide for the group during the hours she wasn't occupied with the cooking school. Jane hoped that didn't mean Hillary would do the driving.

It was a good idea, but Billy should have come up with it sooner. One week before they had to put down a deposit on the house, Hillary only had two people sign up: Henry McEdwards, a local accountant, and his wife, Lola.

That was not counting Shakura Young, ten years old, and Sarah's best friend. She didn't count because she was sharing a room with Sarah. Jane knew that Thelma Young, Shakura's mother, had to sacrifice just to come up with the airfare, but Thelma was delighted that her daughter had the opportunity to travel.

Two days before the deadline, Hillary had convinced a third, Beau Jackson, the local police chief, who hadn't had a vacation in five years and who, Hillary said, agreed to go only because Jane would be there. Jane had gone out with him once, to dinner and a movie in Montgomery. She'd had a good time and might have gone out with him again if his schedule and her daughter hadn't kept each of them busy.

"You've got to come up with one more person, Jane," Hillary had insisted on the day before she had to fax the reservations to the travel agent. "You can't let this opportunity get by us."

Jane might have argued that she had a mountain of tasks Hillary had already given her that would keep her busy until their departure date. Or she might have argued that it didn't really matter to her, personally, whether or not they stayed in the country house of the Compte de Lenoir. But she didn't. If Hillary was generous enough to pay her expenses to France, as well as Sarah's, she'd come up with one more warm body who had enough cash to help pay the rent.

Buddy Fletcher, an ex-con whom Jim Ed had once successfully defended on a burglary charge, was not her first choice. As it turned out, though, he was her only choice.

Buddy showed up at her house the evening before the deadline. "I was in the neighborhood, so I figured I ought to stop by and see about you," he'd said when she opened the door.

Ever since he'd found out that Jane had once been married to Jim Ed, he'd made seeing after her his special mission, "as a favor to ol' Jim Ed," he said. Jane could never convince him that Jim Ed really didn't care about her welfare. The meager divorce settlement she'd gotten was witness to that.

"Nice of you to stop by, Buddy." Jane held the door open for him, hoping that his being in the neighborhood didn't mean he was plying his trade there.

Buddy was likely to stop by at just about any time. He had no regular job. In fact, he had no visible means of support, but Jane had reason to believe he still had plenty of reason to deal with a certain fence in Montgomery.

He entered, pulling his NRA cap off of his head. His wild-looking, longish hair kept the shape of the cap around his head.

"Ain't looked in on you in a while. Don't want ol' Jim

Ed to think I ain't looking after his woman."

"Buddy, I've told you a hundred times, I am not Jim Ed's—"

"How you been?" Buddy sat down on the sofa, helped himself to a handful of peanuts from a dish on the coffee table, then moved a stack of magazines and pop cans out of his way and propped his feet on the same table. Jane was the antithesis of a domestic goddess.

Jane sighed. "All right, I guess." She didn't have the heart to complain about Buddy's unannounced visits, which so often coincided with dinnertime. He'd helped her out of a tight spot or two, including picking Sarah up at school and delivering her to soccer practice or violin lessons when she couldn't get away, and even loaning her money when her paycheck ran out before the end of the month.

"Where's Sarah?" Buddy was looking around for her.

"Up in her room, packing."

"Packing? For what? You ain't sending her to summer camp, are you?" He wore a look of alarm. "You don't never know what goes on at them places, and I ain't so sure ol' Jim Ed would—"

"She's not going to summer camp, Buddy. She's going with me. To France."

"France?" He sounded alarmed. "You going to France?"

"Yes, we are."

"Ain't that where them Frenchmen come from?"

"I believe it is."

He shook his head, disapproving. "Ain't they the ones that pinches women on the butt?"

"You're thinking of Italians."

"Still . . ."

"Don't worry, Buddy. I'll be well chaperoned," Jane said, anticipating his next tirade about ol' Jim Ed not approving.

"Who you going with?"

"My boss, Hillary. And a group. It's sort of a tour."

"Got room for one more?"

"I'm not sure—"

"Hell, you know what they say. They's always room for one more. Sign me up." He popped another handful of nuts in his mouth.

"Buddy, I—well, you need to know it's rather expensive, and I'm not sure you will enjoy—"

Buddy shook his head and grinned. "That's OK, I can swing it. My profits was off last year, but I decided to diversify. Got a cash crop out there in the woods that's making all the difference." He grinned proudly. Jane didn't dare ask what kind of crop. "Can you get me in?" he asked.

In the end, Jane gave in and told him she'd see what she could do, and fed him dinner besides.

Hillary, who might have balked at the idea of Buddy Fletcher filling the fourth slot, was, as Jane was afraid she'd be, glad to get him. She faxed the information to the travel agent and deposited Buddy's down payment within two hours after she got it.

The plan was to meet at Hillary's place early on the morning of August thirteenth. Hillary and Billy would host a breakfast, planned and prepared by Hillary, of course, and then the group would drive to the airport in Montgomery, where they would board a commuter flight to the Atlanta airport to connect with their flight to Paris.

Jane had just turned her six-year-old Toyota onto the long, shaded driveway of the Scarborough's estate when she met a large sports utility van coming off the driveway onto the street. She caught only a fleeting glance of the robust, burly man who was driving it.

Jane and Sarah, accompanied by Shakura, drove up to the front of the house, parked the Toyota, walked to the house, and rang the doorbell. Sarah was jittery with excitement as they waited.

"Will the maid answer the door, Mom? How can people afford maids, anyway? Even Hillary. I mean, aren't they awfully expensive? Daddy and Leslie don't even have a full-time one." Sarah turned to Shakura. "You won't believe this, but Mrs. Scarborough's maid wears a black dress and a frilly white apron, just like in those old movies!"

"Really?" Shakura said, wide-eyed.

Sarah turned back to Jane. "If Mrs. Scarborough's rich, how come she doesn't have a butler? Do you think the maid will go with us to—"

Sarah's nonstop questions were stopped only after the maid opened the door. She was the perfect servant, smiling in her black dress and frilly white apron and, just to make it even better for Sarah, a little white cap as well.

"This is sooo bad!" Sarah said, staring at her.

Shakura simply stared.

"Y'all come in," the maid said. "Miss Hillary is waiting for you in the drawing room."

Sarah tugged at Jane's hand. "Is Martha here?"

Jane pointed ahead of them. "There she is by the staircase, squatting in that big potted plant."

Sarah rushed toward the little dog at the same time the maid gasped and Hillary came fluttering in, palms up in alarm and wearing a smart plum-colored pant suit with shoes and nails to match and her heavy dark hair perfectly styled. "Oh my Lord, Martha, you have no manners at all! Going potty in my plant!" She swooped the dog up in her arms.

Martha jerked her head toward Jane and growled low in her throat. Hillary thrust the animal toward the maid. "She's pouting because I'm leaving for two weeks," she said, looking at Jane.

"Can we play with her?" Sarah asked. She was already reaching for Martha, who licked her face happily.

"Of course," Hillary said.

"Be careful," Jane said at the same time. Martha snarled at her again, but Sarah, Martha, and Shakura disappeared into the kitchen, along with the maid.

Hillary led Jane to the parlor where their traveling companions were all waiting. Jane was relieved to see that most of them were dressed as casually as she was, with an emphasis on comfort for the long plane trip. She spotted Beau Jackson first, who smiled and gave her a little wave. He looked especially handsome in his jeans and crisp white shirt, open at the collar. A shock of his sandy-colored hair fell across one eyebrow.

Buddy's hair was wet and slicked back from his face, and he held his NRA cap between his knees, which were clad in a stiff new pair of jeans.

Henry McEdwards wore a silk shirt, opened an extra button at the collar to reveal a mass of dark chest hair while the thick, equally dark hair on his head was blow-dried and styled in a pompadour so stiff it looked like porcelain. Lola sat across from him, looking overdressed and overstuffed in a bright yellow sundress and gaudy jewelry.

Hillary fluttered in, her high heels clicking on the highly polished hardwood floors and then sinking into the plush oriental rug as she advanced to the center of the room. "Now that we're all here, I don't think we should delay breakfast one minute longer. We don't want to be late for the plane, do we?"

"I can't believe you're serving breakfast to guests just before you leave on a trip," Jane said.

"But we must get off to a festive start!" Hillary said. "And anyway, I'm keeping it simple. We'll start with champagne, of course, and then poached pears as an appetizer followed by oven-roasted pepper bacon with a vegetable omelet—fresh vegetables from my garden, of course— and hot, crusty bread I baked this morning."

Jane and Lola exchanged raised-eyebrow looks, and Lola whispered, "Do you suppose she laid her own eggs?"

Sarah and Shakura were late coming to the table because Jane insisted that they wash their hands after playing with grumpy Martha. Once they were all seated, the maid served the meal on Wedgewood china. Jane was seated with Sarah on her left and Beau Jackson on her right. Both were staring in bewilderment at the array of Francis I sterling silver forks and spoons in front of them. Buddy, who was across from her, had already picked up a knife and a fork and sat with them grasped in his fists, one on each side of his plate.

A place had been set for Billy at the end of the table, opposite Hillary, but his chair was empty.

"Isn't Billy coming?" Jane asked.

Hillary was unfolding her mint-green linen napkin, specially selected to contrast with the cool blue of the tablecloth. "Oh, you weren't here when he got the telephone call. He had to run down to his office for just a few minutes to put out a brush fire that flared up suddenly. Something to do with one of his international clients. He'll meet us at the airport in Montgomery."

"Ever been to France before, Jackson?" Henry said, smacking his lips after sipping the champagne.

"No, I'm afraid I haven't," Beau answered.

"Man, wait till you see the Riviera!" He wiggled his eyebrows, then glanced at Sarah and Shakura before he cut his eyes back to Beau. "I'll tell you about it later."

"Yeah, I'm sure," Beau said.

"What? What's the big secret?" Buddy was speaking over the chunk of omelet he had in his mouth and glancing from Henry to Beau.

Henry wiggled his eyebrows again. "Never mind."

Buddy wore a frown. It was difficult to tell whether he was confused or angry.

Sarah breathed a deep sigh. "What he's trying to say, Buddy, is that women on the Riviera go topless, but he thinks he shouldn't say it in front of children."

Jane saw Beau try to repress a smile.

Buddy's eyes widened. "Topless? You mean . . ."

Sarah nodded. "Yes, Buddy. No tops to their swimsuits."

Buddy shook his head in disbelief. "No way." He glanced at Jane, who nodded affirmatively.

"Well, hell, it's a good thing you got me along. I know for sure ol' Jim Ed wouldn't approve of—"

"Wonderful omelet!" Jane turned to Hillary. "Have we ever done this one on your show?"

Hillary gave her a puzzled frown. "We just did it last week."

"I don't know about the Riviera," Beau said, "but I'm hoping to get out to the Camargue. That beach where the wild horses are."

Jane glanced at him. "Wild horses? Really?" Beau raised horses of his own, which had quickly endeared him to Sarah.

"Can me and Shakura go, too?" Sarah asked.

"We'll see," Jane said.

"Is there any shopping anywhere close by where we're staying?" Lola asked.

"I don't know about shopping, but wait until you see the cooking school. It's small but very prestigious," Hillary said.

"I read in the travel brochure about a nice little restaurant in a town called Arles," Beau said. "If you can get away, Jane, I'd like to take you there."

"Mom, can I have some champagne?" Sarah was offering her glass to the maid, who was pouring another round.

"Why yes, that would be lovely, if—absolutely not!"

"I ain't so sure ol' Jim Ed—"

"Hey, Jackson, it's a good thing we got Buddy along with us. That ought to keep the crime rate down in Prosper while we're—"

Another snap of the napkin. "Henry! Really!"

"If you like the poached pears, keep in mind they can be baked in a filo crust and served with chocolate syrup as a dessert," Hillary said to no one in particular.

Jane felt relief when breakfast was finally over and Hillary announced that it was time to leave. Beau convinced her to leave her Toyota parked at Hillary's place and ride with him to the airport.

"Interesting group," Beau said, helping Jane into the car.

"I'm not sure that's the right word," Jane said.

It was a pleasant enough ride, and Jane was glad for the excuse not to ride with Hillary, whose erratic driving habits left her unnerved as well as a little amazed that she'd had neither a serious accident nor a traffic ticket. She did, however, back her Cadillac into a sculpted juniper as she left, then drove off, oblivious to the fact that she carried away a sizable branch in her bumper.

During the drive to Montgomery, Sarah and Shakura read aloud to each other from a children's suspense novel by Madge Harrah, and Jane and Beau had a relaxed conversation. Jane marveled at how Beau could be conversant about everything from his twin hobbies of horses and prize-winning roses to criminology and the philosophy of Kant. Most of her conversations lately had been with Sarah or other ten-year-olds or Buddy Fletcher or Hillary.

Jane felt relaxed for the first time in weeks as she walked into the airport, holding Shakura's hand on one side and Sarah's on the other while Beau saw to their luggage.

She went straight to the gate area to wait for him and found Hillary and the others already there. Hillary hurried to her side as soon as she saw her.

"Jane! I have to talk to you." She pulled her aside.

"What is it, Hillary?"

"That man over there."

Jane turned around to glance at the man Hillary was staring at. He sat at a table in the airport's McDonald's concession several yards away "What about him?"

"I can't see him clearly, but I think he looks suspicious."

"Why, because he's eating a Quarter Pounder? That's what most people eat, Hillary. Instead of poached pears."

"Quarter Pounder? A quarter pound of what?"

"Never mind. It's all right. I don't think there's anything to worry about."

"I think he's following me."

"And why do you think that?"

"Because everywhere I go, he goes. He was right behind me when we left Prosper. He followed me right up to the airport parking lot, and then he got out of his car and followed me into the terminal."

Jane shook her head. "There's nothing unusual about that, Hillary. A lot of people in Prosper come to the Montgomery airport."

Before Hillary could reply, her name was called on the airport paging system, a female voice telling her to pick up a white courtesy phone. A few minutes later, just before the boarding began, she came back.

"Billy's been delayed," she said, gathering up her carry-on bag. "He'll come on a later flight and meet us in France."

In the next moment, they were all standing with the other passengers in a cluster near the boarding gate. If Sarah hadn't left her book on the seat in the waiting area and gone back to retrieve it, Jane would never have turned around to keep an eye on her, and if she hadn't turned around, she would never have seen Henry McEdwards talking to the man who had been eating the Quarter Pounder and then surreptitiously hand him something that he pulled from beneath a newspaper. The man took it and walked away.

About eight hours later—after what seemed an endless flight to Paris—Jane saw the man again. He seemed to be watching them, and then he ducked away quickly behind a cart full of luggage and disappeared into the crowd in the Charles de Gaulle Airport.

2

"That man! Isn't he the one we saw at the airport in Montgomery?" Jane leaned toward Hillary to speak while she clutched Sarah's hand on one side and Shakura's on the other and at the same time tried to balance a carry-on bag on her shoulder.

Jane's eyes stung from lack of sleep. Traveling in the coach section made sleep impossible, she'd found. Hillary, who'd been in the first-class section, didn't look much better, however.

Sarah and Shakura had slept the sound sleep of the young and innocent and bubbled with excitement as they chattered to each other.

"What man?" Hillary asked.

"I think I saw him, too," Beau said. "It looked like Paul Hayes."

Jane glanced at Beau, surprised. "You know him?"

"Paul Hayes? Why of course we know him," Hillary said. "His family's been in banking in Prosper for years. Belongs to Billy's lodge. Is that who was following me? I never could see him clearly."

"He wasn't following you, Hillary, he was just . . . Lodge? What lodge?" Jane was almost too tired to focus her thoughts.

"The Masons, lamb. Billy's a past Grand Master."

"Is Henry a member, too?" Henry and Lola had moved away from the group to a money exchange machine.

Hillary was signaling a sky cap to help her with her luggage. "I don't know, but I'm sure he is. I mean, everybody who's anybody belongs to the Masons."

"I ain't never joined," Buddy said. He glanced at Beau, who shrugged and shook his head.

Hillary frowned. "Well, I think it's just plain tacky that he showed up here. If he was coming to France at this time, he could have joined my group."

"Tell Billy. Maybe he can get him kicked out of the lodge for that," Jane said.

Hillary eyed her suspiciously. "Are you making fun of me, Jane?"

"Make fun of you, cherie? You're my bread and butter, Hillary. Or make that my croissant and café."

Within the next few moments, Jane had forgotten about Paul Hayes as she and Beau went looking for a taxi driver who could speak English well enough to get them to the hotel where they'd spend a few hours catching up on lost sleep before they boarded a train for Avignon the next morning.

It was late by the time they arrived in Avignon, where Hillary had rented a van big enough to transport the entire group.

"Oh dear, all of the street signs are in French!" she said as they pulled out of the rental lot.

"You're driving on the wrong side of the road!" Beau said.

Hillary waved a hand at him. "Nonsense. Everybody drives on the wrong side of the road over here."

"They do?" Buddy sounded shocked.

"Hell no, they don't!" Henry said as a truck turned onto the street headed straight for their car.

"It's England where they drive on the wrong side!" Jane screeched.

Hillary swerved just in time to miss the truck. "Are you sure?"

"Trust me," Jane said.

"Maybe I should drive," Beau said.

Hillary ignored him. She had, by now, turned onto a roundabout, and she was making the circle on the van's two left wheels.

"You should have turned at the last exit," Jane said.

"This is just like a carnival ride," Shakura said, and Sarah giggled in response.

"You're a hell of a driver," Buddy said.

"Let me drive!" said Beau.

"Mother of God!" said Lola, crossing herself.

"Shit!" said Henry.

By this time, Hillary had circled the roundabout for the third time, and this time managed to take the proper exit.

"Isn't this fun?" Hillary was beaming with excitement.

There was a long moment of stunned silence. Even Sarah and Shakura were wide-eyed and speechless.

When they had left town and were traveling through the countryside, Hillary drove as if she was in the Grand Prix.

"By God, Hillary, if you don't slow down, I'm going to have to arrest you!" Beau shouted.

Hillary waved her perfectly manicured hand at him. "Oh pooh! You're out of your jurisdiction. And besides, I'm not even up to the speed limit yet." She turned around to talk to him in the backseat. "I just saw a sign that said one hundred twenty-five. They do drive fast here, don't they?"

"You're going off the road!" Jane screamed.

Hillary turned around and righted the car with a jerk.

"Besides," Jane added. "The speed limit sign was in kilometers per hour, not miles."

"To convert kilometers to miles, divide by eight and multiply by five," Sarah and Shakura said together.

"Or you can multiply by point six," Beau said.

"Well for heaven's sake, how is a person supposed to remember that? Why don't they just put the signs in miles per hour?" Hillary sounded perturbed, but she had at least slowed down.

"Because we're in France, Hillary," Jane said. "We're not in Kansas anymore."

Hillary seemed not to hear. "Now that you mention it, I remember Billy saying something about dividing by six."

"That's to convert francs to dollars." Jane was holding onto the seat with both hands, not daring to take her eyes off the road.

"Oh." Hillary looked confused.

"And another thing you have to get used to," Jane added, "is temperature measured in centigrade. I forgot the formula for converting it to Fahrenheit."

"Divide by five, multiply by nine, and add thirty-two," Sarah and Shakura said together.

"Do what?" Buddy said.

"My, my," Hillary said.

"Watch that curve!" Jane and Beau said.

It took thirty hair-raising minutes for the group to arrive at the château of the Compte de Lenoir just outside of the village of Lenoir. After a drive through a shadowed lane, the house loomed in front of them, a massive stone giant grown dark with age and sprouting turrets and spires. Yet, in spite of its age, the building still maintained an air of grand elegance. Gargoyles crouched near the roof and at the front of the stone steps, looking as if they were ready to pounce. Stone arches above the windows were hewn with intricate designs, and the wide wooden doors, heavy and encrusted with ironwork, had the look of aristocratic antiquity.

Hillary's hand fluttered to her mouth. "Oh my Lord, it's beautiful."

"It is," Jane agreed.

Hillary frowned slightly. "But the garden's a bit unkempt. Those trees should be trimmed and the shrubs shaped. And I think some nice bulbs in pots around the edge there would be the perfect touch. Bulbs do well in a Mediterranean climate, you know. I'd suggest, oh, maybe amaryllis or paperwhite narcissus. What do you think, Jane?"

"Huh? Oh yeah, sure," Jane said, not having any idea what an amaryllis or a paperwhite narcissus was. The only thing she'd ever been able to grow was mildew in the bathroom, but she figured it was part of her job as Hillary's assistant to at least pretend an interest.

"Let us out of the car; we want to explore!" Sarah said from the back.

"It's so cool. Just like a house in a fairy tale," Shakura said.

Lola had already started for the front door. "I can't wait to see the inside."

Henry was pulling suitcases out of the back. "Come on! Everybody help unload the stuff."

Buddy pushed his NRA cap back on his head and looked around. "I'll get my stuff out in a minute. I think I'll just check out the neighborhood first."

Jane cut her eyes quickly toward Beau and back to Buddy. "You're on vacation now, Buddy. Forget about work."

"Who said anything about work? I was just going to—"

Jane nodded. "I know, Buddy, I know. I've seen you check out a neighborhood before. Just stay out of trouble, OK?"

"Now, Miz Ferguson—"

"Help me with my bags, Buddy. It's what Jim Ed would want."

"Well, sure." He picked up four bags, one under each arm and one in each hand, and started up the long path to the house.

"Jim Ed?" Beau said.

"That always distracts him," Jane said. "He thinks he has to take care of me for Jim Ed."

"Doesn't he know you're—"

"Divorced? Sure, he knows. Don't try to understand the way a mind like that works."

Beau laughed. "Here, I'll help you with that last bag. Let's go find our rooms."

Hillary had already unlocked the front door, and she and the others were inside. Hillary was reading off room assignments. "The maids will be in every morning to make the beds and do the cleaning, but we're on our own for meals. Of course, I can't wait to share with you some of the cuisine I'll be creating. Breakfast will be at seven every morning and dinner at eight, except tonight, we'll eat at six-thirty."

She sounded like a camp counselor, but no one seemed to mind. Everyone, including Jane, was eager to settle into their rooms. Jane had been assigned a beautiful room decorated in tones of deep rose and green with a canopy bed that looked somehow decadent and risqué. Shakura and Sarah were in an adjoining room with a bathroom in between.

Jane had almost everything unpacked when the two girls came running into her room. Sarah was flushed with anticipation, and Shakura's dark face had taken on an excited glow.

"Mrs. Scarborough is going to love this place, Mom, there are acres and acres of gardens," Sarah said.

"And a stable with horses," Shakura added.

"Wonderful. Maybe Beau can arrange to take you two riding while Hillary and I are in cooking class." Jane was absorbed with shaking the wrinkles out of a skirt.

"I can't believe you're taking a cooking class, Mom."

"Why not?"

"Because you hate to cook."

"It's my job, sweetie. It pays the bills."

Shakura giggled. "My mom says Mrs. Scarborough

couldn't make it without you. She says you keep her organized because you're so smart. She says you should go back to school and finish your law degree."

Jane slipped a blouse on a hanger. "One of these days." She turned to Sarah and Shakura. "You girls go unpack now."

"Can't we wait until later?" Sarah pleaded. "We want to explore some more. There's a church or something out there that looks really old, and a farmhouse and another building that must be where they make wine."

Jane gently led the girls back to their room. "All of that will be there tomorrow, and the next day, and every day for the next two weeks. There'll be plenty of time to explore."

The girls finally agreed, reluctantly, to finish their unpacking. Jane had unpacked her own bags and was about to settle onto the high canopy bed for a rest when she heard a knock at her door. She got up to open it.

"Beau!"

He stood in her doorway, grinning and looking boyish in his white shirt and jeans with tennis shoes. "Hillary has us segregated. Boys on one side of the house, girls on the other. Just like summer camp." He peeked around Jane's shoulder. "Right nice place you have here."

"Isn't yours?"

"Sure. Looks like a hunting lodge. Got the head of an ibex or something over my bed and racks of antique guns."

"Oh how masculine."

"Do I detect a note of cynicism?"

"Perhaps."

He grinned. "Want to go for a walk?"

"Sure. I'll just tell the girls."

"The girls are already gone. I saw them skipping down the hall as I came."

"Well, then, let's go," she said. "There seems to be plenty to see, according to those two. We can go see the winery and maybe the chapel they told me about."

The sun had begun to slip low in the sky behind them as they walked along the long shaded path. A soft breeze made the air balmy—a comfortable contrast to sweltering Alabama. Beau glanced at Jane. "Who would have thought I'd ever be in France with Jane Ferguson?"

"Who would have thought Jane Ferguson would ever be in France?"

"Well, I'm glad you're here." With his Southern accent, he always pronounced the word *heah*. "I've wanted to get you alone someplace like this ever since I met you."

Jane gave him a surprised look. "Why Beaumont Jackson! Are you coming on to me?"

He grinned and seemed about to say something else, but they were both distracted by a voice calling to them from somewhere up the path.

"Miz Ferguson, is that you?"

Jane sighed. "Yes, Buddy, it's me."

He was hurrying toward them. "Do you think you ort to be out here alone in a foreign country when it's getting late?"

"It's not late, Buddy." Jane said.

"She's not alone," Beau said at the same time.

Buddy stopped in front of them, puffing from walking too fast. "Well, what are y'all doing?"

"Nothing now, that's for sure," Beau said.

"Huh?"

"Just taking a walk," Jane said.

"Then I'll just come along with you, just to make sure nothing happens to you."

"Don't trouble yourself, Buddy. I'll be all right. Really." Jane glanced at Beau and saw him give a resigned shrug.

"Oh, it ain't no trouble. What are we going to do?"

Beau extended an arm down the road. "Whatever you want, Buddy. Just lead the way."

A slight frown creased Buddy's forehead. "I ain't never had a cop say that to me before." He hesitated only a moment. "Well, hell, let's just see how far we can go."

"That's pretty much what I had in mind before you showed up," Beau said.

Buddy turned away just long enough for Jane to give Beau a warning nudge with her elbow before the three of them started down the path again.

They found the winery first, an ancient brick building covered with vines and shaded by tall trees. A sign in front said it was the Mas du Compte. The wide front door was standing open, and a ruddy-faced young man waved to them from the inside.

"Bonjour!" he called.

"Bonjour," Jane replied, using practically the only French she knew.

Buddy looked confused. "Say what?"

"Ah, you are Americans," the young man said, walking toward them. "Staying in the château, perhaps?"

"That's right," Beau said.

The young man extended his hand. "I am Guillaume Daudet. Welcome to Provence. Welcome to Mas du Compte."

"Merci," Beau said, making it sound like *mercy.* Jane got the feeling he had just used all the French he knew as well.

"You would like a tour of the winery, *n'est-ce pas? Un petit* taste of the wine?"

"That guy talks funny," Buddy said, under his breath to Jane.

"Sure," Jane said, ignoring Buddy. "I mean, *oui.*"

The tour of the winery was fascinating to Jane from the mechanical crusher that delicately separated the grapes from their stems to the fermenting vats and the cool, damp tunnel where the wine was stored in wooden casks before it was bottled, and the candling room where the ancient technique of holding the bottle over a candle to look for cloudiness or sediment was still practiced.

After the tour, Guillaume offered them a private tasting of six of his wines. By the time they had sampled each wine three times, the chardonnay tasted exactly like the claret to Jane, and her nose was numb.

"You got any beer?" Buddy asked.

Guillaume was too absorbed with being a tour guide to answer his question. Jane was ready to go back to the château for a long, hot bath, but Guillaume insisted that they also see the tiny chapel on the grounds of the winery.

"It was built eight hundred years ago by the Knights Templar and dedicated to Saint Denis in gratitude for their safe return from the Holy Land. Now it is only used for the marriages and special holy days, but once it was used for the secret ceremonies of the Templars."

"Secret?" Buddy said. "Was they up to something fishy?"

Guillaume looked confused. *"Je ne comprend pas,* 'up to something fishy.' "

"Say what?"

"Never mind, Buddy," Jane said. Or tried to say. Her tongue was a little thick.

Buddy took off his cap and held it close to his chest as he entered the chapel.

The chapel was tiny and dark, with a stone floor and stone walls and a small altar at the end of the room. A few primitive icons hung on the walls. A door to the side of the altar was closed and secured with a lock and chain.

"Interesting," Beau said.

Buddy twisted his cap. "I ain't been in a church in a long time. Feels kind of creepy."

Jane hiccuped.

When they got back to the château, Hillary was waiting for them in the front hall. She looked distressed.

"I have bad news," she said.

A knot formed in Jane's stomach. "Oh my God, has something happened to Sarah and Shakura?"

Hillary shook her head. "Oh no, lamb, they're fine. I sent them to their room to get ready for dinner. I had a telegram from Billy. He can't make it until next week."

"Why am I not surprised?" Jane said, weaving slightly. "I'd better go see about the girls." Jane had already started toward the wing where her bedroom was located.

"Don't be long," Hillary called after her. "Dinner will be ready at six-thirty."

Jane turned around. "How can you do that, Hillary? Make dinner after such a long trip?"

"It's nothing, really. I arranged to have the kitchen stocked before we came, and besides, I made a simple meal. We're having beef tenderloin with shallots and red wine glaze and vegetables grilled in olive oil and fresh strawberries for dessert."

"You got any beer?" Buddy asked.

Jane didn't stick around to hear Hillary's reply. She hurried to her room, still hoping for time for a bath.

Sarah was just getting out of the tub when she reached their rooms. Jane hurried her out of the bathroom and ran fresh water into the tub. She had just started to get undressed when she heard a knock at the door.

"Jane! It's me, open up!" It was Hillary's voice, breathless and excited. Jane hurried to the door.

"Come in, Hillary. What's going on?"

Hillary rushed into the room. "Oh my Lord, the worst has happened."

"Let me guess. Billy's not coming at all."

"No, no, of course he's coming. It's something worse."

Jane thought she might faint. Whether from the wine or from Hillary's distressed look, she wasn't sure. "For heaven's sake, Hillary, what's wrong?"

"I don't have any red wine to go with tonight's meal. What am I going to do?"

Jane sat down heavily on the bed, her heart pounding. "Good Lord, Hillary, you had me scared. I thought it was a real emergency."

"It *is* a real emergency. What am I going to do?"

"Take a deep breath, Hillary. Relax. You're just going to have to buy a bottle of red wine. Now, is that so hard?"

"Of course it is. All the stores are sure to be closed by the time I can get into the village, and even if they're not, it will take too long. The beef will be ruined!"

"How about the winery? They'll sell you some."

For the first time, Hillary's face brightened. "Do you think they would still be open?"

"They were just a moment ago."

Hillary was holding the door open. "Then let's go. Hurry!"

"Can't you go by yourself, Hillary? I still have to take a bath and—"

"Of course I can't go by myself. I need you with me."

"But why? It's just a short walk. Turn right at the end of the long driveway, and cross the street at—"

Hillary put her fingertips to her temples. "I can't remember all that in my state. You *must* go with me!"

Jane breathed a deep sigh of resignation and stood up. She walked through the bathroom and tapped on Sarah and Shakura's door. "I'm going out with Hillary. Be back in a minute." She took a few minutes to wash her face with cold water, hoping it would clear her head of the fuzziness the wine had caused.

"I want a lovely Côtes du Rhône," Hillary said as the walked along the path. "Red wine is absolutely essential with French food, you know."

Jane's only comment was a noncommittal "Mmm," since she wasn't at all sure what a Côtes du Rhône was and because her mind was on the hot bath she hoped she would still have time for.

When they reached the winery, the heavy wooden door was still open, but there were no lights inside the building.

Hillary's hand went to her forehead in one of her most dramatic gestures. "You don't suppose they've gone already."

Jane peered around the door. "Guillaume?" There was no answer. She stepped inside and called his name again. Still there was no answer.

At first all she saw were the half-filled bottles of wine she and Beau and Buddy had tasted. Then, when she turned her head, she saw that the lid to the stainless steel vat where the wine was being processed was open. That was when she saw the corpse, floating faceup, arms spread.

The face was awash with red wine, but she recognized it immediately.

Hillary leaned forward for a better look. "Oh my Lord, that's Paul Hayes! What's a Baptist doing in a wine vat?"

3

Jane was still looking at the body, unable to believe her eyes. Her heart was a relentless hammer inside her chest, and for a moment, she felt again as if she might faint.

Hillary was shaking her head. "You know, I'll bet that's some kind of inferior rosé."

"Geez, Hillary, now's not the time to be a wine snob. The poor guy didn't get to choose the vat they threw him in after he was murdered." Jane's voice sounded choked.

"Don't say that word, Jane!"

Jane ignored her. "He must have been strangled. See those bruises on his neck?"

"Oh Jane, I don't want to think about it." Hillary looked over her shoulder. "Can't we just get out of here, and—"

"And pretend it didn't happen? Hillary, you have an annoying way of sticking your head in the sand." Jane's own head was pounding. She was no longer tipsy, but the wine was giving her a headache.

"Well . . ." Hillary looked as if she was about to cry, and Jane was torn between comforting her and screaming from the horror she felt at the body staring at them through the murky wine.

She took a deep breath. "We have to tell someone. The police. Yes, we have to tell the police."

Hillary was wringing her hands, trying not to look at the body. "Can't we just let the locals take care of it? For all you know, this may be a local custom."

"Someone must have killed him, Hill." Jane's voice was shrill. "I mean people don't just jump in wine vats fully clothed, I don't care how weird their customs are." Her eyes swept the room, searching the deepening shadows.

Hillary sucked in her breath. "Oh my, you don't suppose whoever did it is still . . . ?" She glanced over her shoulder and grabbed Jane's hand. "Let's get out of here," she said in a hoarse whisper.

Just as she spoke, Jane heard a strange creaking sound and then a thud.

Hillary grabbed her around the waist. "What was that?"

"Someone just closed the front door."

"It could have been the wind." Hillary's voice was a hopeful whisper.

"There's no wind."

Hillary let go of Jane and put her face in her hands. "Oh my God! We're alone in a darkened building with a floating dead man."

Jane was ignoring her and had already started for the door.

Hillary hurried after her. "Where are you going, Jane? Don't leave me alone!"

Jane pushed hard on the door, then banged on it with her fists, but it was as solid as the wall. "It's locked!"

"It can't be locked!" Hillary tried to push it open, and when it wouldn't move, she dropped her head on her extended arm. "This can't be happening to me. The beef tenderloin has to come out of the oven in ten minutes."

Jane was just about to tell her that this was not the time to be worrying about beef tenderloin, but before she could speak, they both heard the noise: a subtle thud, like something striking the sides of a wooden barrel.

"What was that?" Hillary whispered.

Jane pressed herself against the wooden door, as if she were trying to will herself to pass through it.

They heard it again, another soft thud, and then a scraping sound.

"You should never have insisted that we come here!" Hillary whispered.

"I shouldn't have insisted? I wasn't the one who—"

"I suggested a store. You insisted on the winery, and look where it's gotten us!"

Jane closed her eyes and tried counting to ten, but her heart was racing so fast it distracted her. She gave up on trying to calm herself and took a step into the vast darkness of the winery.

"Where are you going?" Another urgent whisper.

"We've got to find a way out of here," Jane replied, whispering over her shoulder.

"But what if we run into whoever is making those noises?" Hillary had caught up with her and was walking next to her now.

"I'm not sticking around and waiting for him to find us."

"But . . ."

"I think I remember a window over there to the left. Maybe we can escape through there."

Hillary held on to Jane's arm as they groped their way through the darkness, stumbling over cases of wine. Hillary fell to her knees once, and Jane helped her up. Jane could see the window in front of them and a splash of anemic moonlight shining through the glass.

"Oh Lord," Hillary said, "I'll have to change before dinner. I think I got a smudge on my—"

Jane clasped a hand over Hillary's mouth before she could finish. Someone passed between them and the window. Jane pulled Hillary down with her to crouch behind a row of wine casks. Now it appeared as if whoever it was, was headed toward them, guided by the noise they had made stumbling over the cases of wine.

Still crouching, Jane pulled off one of her sneakers and tossed it to her left. She saw the figure turn his head toward the noise as the sneaker hit the floor, then move toward the sound. Jane grabbed Hillary's hand and raced to the window. It was a large window, at least four feet high and two feet across.

As soon as they reached it, Jane tried to raise the sash, but the heavy wooden frame wouldn't budge.

"Stand back!" Hillary whispered.

Before Jane could collect herself, Hillary had pushed her aside and hit the big single pane with something, sending the glass shattering to the ground outside the window. In the next moment, Hillary was out the window. "Watch out for the broken glass on your bare foot," Hillary said, reaching back in to hold Jane's hand as she helped her through the opening. At the same time, she was replacing the stylish lizard-skin pump on her right foot. The two-inch heel had been the tool she'd used to shatter the window.

Jane managed to hop on one foot until she was clear of the glass, then she ran as hard and fast as she could, wearing only one shoe, back toward the château. Hillary kept up with her. The lizard-skin pumps didn't slow her down at all.

Once they were inside the wide front doors, Jane leaned with her back against them, trying to catch her breath. "Where's the telephone in this place?"

Hillary shook her head. "There isn't one. Remember? That's supposed to be part of the charm. No intrusions from the outside world."

Jane closed her eyes. "Oh, God!" She opened them again, looking at Hillary, still breathing hard. "Then we've got to find one somewhere. A pay phone, or—"

Hillary was walking away from her, headed toward the kitchen. "We don't have time."

"Hillary, we have to—"

"I can't let that lovely beef go to waste."

"For Christ's sake, Hillary, this is more important than your lovely beef."

Hillary whirled around to face her, and Jane saw the troubled look on her face. "Look, Jane, I've announced dinner at six-thirty tonight. We have to go through with that. We can't upset the others with this, now, can we?"

"No, I still think—"

"Do you want Sarah and Shakura to be upset by this? To have nightmares?"

The mention of Sarah and Shakura gave Jane pause. Was Hillary being thoughtful or merely manipulative? It didn't matter. The truth was, she didn't want the girls upset.

"We'll steal away later and call the police. After dinner."

Jane shook her head. "I could do it now, while you serve the dinner. You don't wait to notify the police of these things."

"And what will I say to the girls?"

"Tell them I'm taking a walk." She had already started upstairs to change shoes.

"Jane!" Hillary's voice was edged with panic. "Jane!" she cried again.

Jane stopped, turned around, an annoyed frown creasing her face. "What?"

"I'm going with you."

"What about your lovely beef?"

Hillary still looked troubled. "I know, I know. I'll never forgive you for this, Jane, but I can't let you be wandering around in the night alone with a killer loose."

"Why, Hillary, I'm touched," Jane said and meant it, in spite of the slightly sarcastic note in her voice.

"Just let me go turn off the oven, then I'll try to slip out without anyone seeing me, and I'll meet you in the front. No point in upsetting the others."

Jane nodded. "All right, but hurry." She changed her shoes quickly, then exited the château and closed the heavy doors behind her, thinking it would be best not to be seen in the front hall by one of the other guests. She didn't want to have to answer questions or make excuses for leaving.

As she waited for Hillary, she thought she heard the
sound of someone walking, crunching the gravel on the
long path that led from the road to the château, and she
moved into the shadows of the shrubbery that lined the path
near the house.

She could feel the blood surging through her veins and
pounding in her head as she waited, afraid of who it might
be, who might have followed her from the winery. She
almost cried from relief when the figure finally materialized
in the shadows in front of her.

It was only Lola, dressed in running shoes and garish
pink nylon jogging shorts that made her look even more
plump. Her short hair was pushed back from her face with
an equally garish pink and purple headband. She jogged up
to the front door, puffing and sweating, and slipped her key
into the door.

"This better be worth it," she mumbled to herself as she
wiped sweat from her forehead with the back of her hand.

In the next moment, the door slammed behind her, and
Jane breathed a sigh of relief that it had been only Lola
and not some unknown killer stalking her. The thought
made her reluctant to emerge from her hiding place in the
shrubbery, however, and she was still lurking there when
the front door opened again and Hillary emerged.

Hillary stood with her hands on her hips, looking around
in the growing darkness. "Jane? Are you out here?"

Jane stepped forward. "I'm here."

Hillary seemed startled. "Good Lord, what are you doing
lurking in the bushes?"

"I'll explain later. What took you so long?"

"I had to get the car keys." Hillary dangled them in front
of her. "I thought it would be best if we drove into the
village instead of walking, considering what we just saw."

"Good idea, Hill, but let me drive."

"Oh, it's no trouble." Hillary was already headed for the
van. "Now tell me why you were hiding in the shrubs."

She stopped and looked at Jane, her eyes wide. "Oh dear, you didn't see someone suspicious, did you?"

Jane shook her head. "No, it turned out to be just Lola, but when I heard her jogging up the path, I was afraid it might be whoever that was bumping around in the winery."

"Lola! I saw her, too. Some nerve that woman has to be out jogging so late. If it hadn't been for that dead man in the wine vat, she would have been late for my dinner."

"Some people have all the luck."

"Don't be sarcastic, Jane."

"You didn't talk to Lola, did you?" Jane said, ignoring Hillary's comment. "I mean, as you said, I don't want any word of this getting back to the girls and upsetting them. Maybe we should tell Beau. But later."

"Of course I didn't talk to her." Hillary sounded indignant. "I know how to handle this kind of thing, which is fortunate, since you keep getting us into these messes."

"What do you mean, I keep get us into messes? You're the one who seems to attract trouble. I never had so much excitement in my life until I met you."

"I could say the same thing about you, Jane Ferguson, and I might add, it's not the kind of excitement I care for."

"Well, I don't exactly relish finding dead men in wine vats, if that's what you mean. Give me the keys, Hillary, it's my turn to drive."

Hillary was already unlocking the driver's side door to the van. "Nonsense, you're too upset to drive, and besides, you've been drinking. You'd better let me."

"Hillary, that was hours ago, and . . ."

It was too late to protest. Hillary was already in the driver's seat and had the motor started. Jane had no choice but to go around to the passenger's side and get into the van.

Hillary pulled out of the driveway with a bouncy jerk because she was having trouble shifting into the correct gear, then lurched down the front path, spewing gravel behind her.

"Where do we find a pay phone?" Hillary asked as she drove.

Jane was holding onto the seat with white-knuckled hands. "I have no idea. We'll just have to watch for one. Or ask someone. Watch that bicycle, Hillary!"

The tires squealed as Hillary swerved to keep from hitting the cyclist, and Jane's side pressed into the armrest as she was thrown sideways. She glanced at the man on the bicycle and could just make out in the semidarkness the third-finger salute he gave them as they passed.

Hillary seemed oblivious to all of it. "Why don't you just ask someone where the police station is? We could go directly there, and you could talk to them while I wait in the van."

Jane looked at her wide-eyed. "Me? Talk to them? I'm not the one who speaks French, you do. And what do you mean, wait in the van?"

Hillary waved her beautifully manicured hand. "Why, I don't speak a word of French, lamb. You'll have to do it."

"Of course you speak French! Didn't you name your business Élégance du Sud? Aren't you always throwing around phrases like *gôut rafine* and *trés élégant?*"

Hillary took her eyes off the road to give her a look of disgruntled impatience. "Well, just because I say something doesn't mean I know what it means." She sounded as if she thought that made perfect sense, then glanced at the road again and had to slam on her brakes to keep from hitting a small car.

Jane gave her another look of disbelief while she righted herself again. "Well, I certainly don't speak French. When I first applied for the job with you, I thought Élégance du Sud meant elegant suds, that you ran a laundry or something."

"Oh don't worry, you'll think of something." Hillary was squinting at something in front of them, then she turned suddenly, throwing Jane off balance again.

"For heaven's sake, Hillary, what are you doing?"

"Well, there was nothing on that street that looked like either a pay phone or a police station, so I thought I'd see what's down this street."

The street was barely wide enough for one car and was walled on each side by ancient, three-story row houses. As Hillary hurled the oversized vehicle along the street meant only for horses and carts, neighbors who had been standing in the street talking and visiting had to press themselves against their houses to keep from being run over. They gestured and shouted in French as Hillary careened down the street.

"Hillary! My God!" Jane braced her arms against the dashboard.

"What is it, Jane?" Hillary sounded impatient, annoyed.

"You're going the wrong way! Look!" In front of them was a small European car. It seemed to be wobbling, as if the driver was trying to decide which way to turn to avoid hitting Hillary's van.

Hillary slammed on her brakes just as the two vehicles met, nose to nose, with only a fraction of an inch of space between bumpers. The driver of the small car, a man of perhaps forty-five, dressed in jeans and a neatly pressed shirt, jumped out of the car, shouting and gesturing as he walked up to Hillary's window.

Hillary simply smiled at him and said, "Well, my Lord, that was close, wasn't it?"

The driver, who Jane could see had a rugged, handsome face, was waving his arms and screaming, *"Est-ce-que vous êtes idiote? Regardez! C'es sens unique!"* He pointed in the opposite direction in which Hillary's van was headed.

Hillary stuck her head out her window and gave the man a friendly wave. "That's right nice of you, lamb!"

"What did he say?" Jane asked.

Hillary shook her head. "I don't know. I didn't understand a word. These Frenchmen are so excitable! But he just had to have been telling me he was going to back up and let me pass."

By now, several people had crowded around the two vehicles, talking and gesturing. Although Jane couldn't understand what they were saying, it wasn't difficult to understand their gestures.

"They're trying to tell you this is a one-way street, and you're going the wrong way," Jane said, "and I think you're wrong about that guy in front of us offering to back up." She was looking at the way his face had grown redder and the way he was shaking his fist at the two of them.

"Well, he doesn't expect me to back up, does he?"

"I think he does, Hillary." Jane was growing more and more tense, especially since the man was walking toward them and wildly waving his fist.

"Oh!" Hillary obviously had seen him as well. She shifted into what she thought was reverse. It was third. The van lurched forward, hitting the bumper of the car in front of her, then sputtered and died. The angry man was by now standing next to Hillary's window. She looked at him and gave him a smile. "I'm not used to a stick shift," she said.

"Est-ce-que vous avez appris à conduire dans un asile d'aliénés?" He waved his hands wildly, and his face had grown even more red.

"Thank you, hon. You have a nice day, too, hear?"

Hillary glanced at Jane. "I think he wants to back my van up for me."

Jane shook her head. "I don't think that's what he—"

The man opened the door suddenly, and Jane felt her heart drop.

"My, my, what nice manners. He's opening the door for me, see?" Hillary said, getting out of the van.

"Vous êtes folle, madam! Folle! Et je vous dis que . . . uh . . . que . . . " He eyed Hillary up and down, and his expression had changed from anger to appreciation.

"It is so nice of you to do this for me," Hillary said, giving him her most charming smile.

"Mmmm, oui, oui," the man said, still giving her his admiring appraisal.

"I'm actually an excellent driver, but I'm just not familiar with the neighborhood. You know how that is, and, well, this is kind of a tight spot, isn't it?"

It was her best Southern belle act, and Jane watched it in amazement.

Hillary handed the man her keys and, with elaborate gestures and sign language, finally got across what she wanted.

The man took her keys, then indicated, with his own elaborate gestures, that Hillary was to get in first. Hillary slid in next to Jane, and the man got in next to her.

Hillary turned to Jane. "Everything's going to be just fine."

"Oh, I'm sure it is!"

"This is my assistant, Jane Ferguson," Hillary said.

The man gave her a passing glance, then started the van and shifted the gears. Jane noticed that in the process, his hand brushed Hillary's knee and lingered there a little longer than necessary. Then he put his arm on the back of the seat and turned his head, as if to see behind him better, but his eyes were not on the narrow street; they were on Hillary.

When he had the van backed all the way to the end of the street, he still had not taken his eyes off of Hillary, and his hand brushed her knee once again as he shifted into neutral.

"Oh, I just appreciate this so much!" Hillary's tone was unabashedly gushing. *"Merci! Merci!"*

"Il n'y a pas de quoi, surtout, pour une femme si belle."

"Oh you are so right about that," Hillary said, giving him another of her smiles.

Jane was relieved when the man opened the car door. She'd thought for a moment he might not want to get out, given that he appeared so smitten by Hillary. As he exited, he lifted Hillary's hand and kissed it, and the onlookers responded with oohs and ahs and a bit of good-natured laughter.

"Listen, do any of y'all know where the police station

is?" Hillary called out to the crowd. She had pronounced the word *po*-leese.

Everyone answered her at once. All in French. It wasn't clear whether they were attempting to answer the question or not.

"Well, thank you. To all of y'all!" Hillary gave one of her little waves, threw the van into some undetermined gear, and lurched away, sending more pedestrians to seek refuge flat against the walls of the houses.

Jane righted herself in her seat again. "Well, that was something else, Hillary. I've never seen you do the helpless Southern belle act so well. You were in fine form."

"Well, what else could I do? I just had to pretend I don't know the first thing about driving."

"You do that very well, Hillary."

"Thank you. Now, where do you suppose the police station is?"

They had left the residential section and were once again on the wider thoroughfare. "If they spell police the same way in French as we do in English, I think it's there," Jane said, pointing to a relatively modern-looking building in front of them bearing a sign that read COMISSARET DE POLICE.

"Wonderful!" Hillary said. With a quick jerk on the steering wheel, she turned the van into the parking area in front of the building, knocking over a public trash can and sending it rolling down the drive until it was stopped by the tires of a parked police vehicle. She ignored it, however, and got out of the van and walked in a quick pace to the front door, her high heels clicking on the flagstone walkway. Jane got out of the van and hurried to catch up with her.

There was only a dim light shining from somewhere inside, and the building looked deserted. The door was unlocked, however, and they both stepped inside.

Once they were inside the foyer, Jane could see that the light was coming from an office ahead of them and to the left.

"Hello?" Jane called as she walked toward the office. Hillary was lagging behind her as if she was reluctant to go much farther. "Is anyone here?" Jane called.

"Who is it? May I help you?" The response came in English with a French accent from somewhere inside the lighted room.

Jane felt a rush of relief at hearing the words in English. She started for the office. "Yes, we're two Americans and we'd like to report a—" She stopped in mid-sentence when she saw the man behind the desk.

It was the man who had been on the bicycle Hillary had almost run off the road. The sign on his desk read PRÉFET DE POLICE.

4

"Oh, I'm so glad you speak English," Hillary said, moving in front of Jane.

Jane glanced around at the office, which was sparsely furnished with a desk, a large filing cabinet, and two chairs for visitors. The walls were plastered in white that had grown a bit dingy with age, and the floor was covered with a nondescript tile.

"Jane has something to report," Hillary continued, "and it will be so much better if you understand what she's saying."

Jane opened her mouth to protest that it wasn't just she who had something to report, that it had been the two of them who'd found the body, but before she could say a word, the man behind the desk was standing and speaking to them again.

"I am Edouard Vautrin," he said, extending his hand. His eyes took in both of them. "I am *le préfet.* What you would call chief of police, I think." He glanced down at his casual attire. "Pardon me for not being in uniform, but it is late, *n'est-ce pas?*" He studied their faces briefly. "You are Americans?"

"We're from a little place south of Birmingham." Hillary sounded as if she was setting him straight, as if she wanted to make sure he knew they weren't from someplace North. She placed a rose-tipped hand on her chest, shook her head, and rolled her eyes slightly. "And I tell you what, I am just as nervous and unsettled about this as I can be."

Vautrin indicated two chairs in front of his desk. "Please sit. And yes, I can imagine how upset you must be. I often have American tourist coming in here with the traffic problems." He shook his head. "Some of the drivers are what you call crazy, *n'est-ce pas?* I, myself, had just such an encounter. Some crazy driver tried to kill me with a car while I am riding my bicycle. If I ever find that car again, I will, um, what you call it? Toss the book at them."

Hillary now put both hands, crisscrossed, on her chest. "Well my Lord! This isn't about a traffic problem."

Vautrin seemed mildly surprised. "No?"

"Tell him, Jane."

Jane stifled an urge to strangle Hillary. She glanced at her and then back at Monsieur Vautrin, uncertain of how to begin, silently praying he didn't recognize them. "I, uh, I'm afraid we have a murder to report."

There was a long moment of silence. Jane felt her heart pummel her chest and perspiration form along her hairline.

Vautrin spoke at last. "A murder?"

Jane managed to squeak, "Yes."

Another long silence while Vautrin looked at her, she thought, as if she were an alien creature. Then his hands suddenly flew to the top of his desk, and he patted mounds of paper until he found a notebook, then pulled a pen from a drawer.

"Your names?" His voice sounded stiff and professional. He held the pen poised above the paper.

Hillary glanced quickly at Jane, then back at Vautrin, smiling weakly. "You won't need my name, of course, since I'm not the one who—"

"Your name?" It was more barked than spoken.

"Hillary Scarborough."

He asked her how to spell it, then scribbled quickly.

"Jane Ferguson," Jane said and spelled it for him before he could bark again.

"And where is the body?"

Jane told him about finding the body in the wine vat when they went back to try to buy a bottle of wine, and she told him about seeing someone in the building. She also told him they were staying at the château and that they'd been in the building earlier with Guillaume Daudet, the proprietor, and that there was nothing amiss then. "And I'm afraid we had to break a window in order to escape because the front door was locked," she added as she finished the story.

Vautrin raised his eyes to study her face again, his expression grim. Jane had the distinct feeling that he was going to arrest them for breaking the window.

"This person in the building. You did not see him clearly, *n'est-ce pas?*"

"No. I mean, yes, you're right; no, we didn't." Jane was having a hard time keeping her nerves calm, and although she no longer felt light-headed from the wine she'd drunk earlier, her headache was worsening.

"You are sure there was a body? That someone was dead?"

Jane nodded. "Oh yes, we're sure." Hillary said nothing.

"No other person saw this, this body?"

Jane shook her head.

He asked several more questions. What time was it when they found the body? What time was it when they were in the building the first time? Had they seen anything suspicious outside the building? Did Guillaume Daudet seem disturbed? When was the last time they had seen him?

"There is one more thing," Jane said, when it seemed he had finished with his questioning.

"Qui?"

"The dead person. We, uh, I mean, Hillary, knows him."

He raised his considerable eyebrows. *"Vraiment?"*

Hillary gave Jane an alarmed look. "I didn't know him *that* well.

Vautrin leaned forward. "And how do you know this man?"

Hillary squirmed in her seat a moment before she answered. "Well, I'm sure this doesn't make any difference, but he belongs to my husband's lodge. Back home in Prosper, I mean."

Vautrin raised his eyebrows; whether it was a confused expression or one of alarm, it was hard to tell. "Prosper?"

Hillary nodded. "Prosper, Alabama. Population fifty thousand."

"Ah, *je vois.*" He studied Hillary a moment. "And what else do you know about this man? His name, *peut-être?"*

Hillary frowned and shook her head. "Oh no. His name's not Petra. It's Hayes. Paul Hayes."

Vautrin scribbled again. "Anything more?"

Hillary put the tip of one of her fingers to her lips. "Well, let's see. He's in banking, and he used to be married to a Parker. The Parkers that came over from Georgia after the war, you know? The War Between the States, I mean. But that didn't last long. The marriage, that is. Not the war. But Lord knows, sometimes I think that's still going on, the way some of those Yankees act."

Vautrin looked thoroughly confused now. "Umm, this man. Hayes? He was at war with some Parkers from Georgia?"

Hillary frowned. "Well, I wouldn't call it a war. It was just disagreeable. But you know how those Georgia Parkers can be. Well, maybe you don't. Anyway, I say he was smart to get rid of her. She had their house done in that tacky nouveau riche style you see all over Atlanta."

Vautrin nodded, still looking confused. "Tell me about the—how did you say, lowdge?"

"Oh, the Masons, you mean." Hillary gave him one of her fluttering hand waves. "I can't tell you a thing about that, hon. You know how Masons are. All that secret ritual and I don't know what all."

"Ah, *les Maçons?* And your husband, he is with you?"

"Billy? Oh no. He won't be here for another few days."

"You have had contact with Monsieur Hayes since you arrived? Other than finding his body, perhaps?"

Hillary looked incensed. "Why, of course not. He should have been the one to contact me, if he was coming to France."

Vautrin looked puzzled again. *"Pardon?"*

Jane was becoming worried that Hillary was going to get them in even more trouble. "Uh, what she means is, no we haven't had any contact with Mr. Hayes, but . . ." Jane felt uneasy and was uncertain how to continue.

The look on Vautrin's face was one of interested anticipation. He made a rolling motion with his hand, urging her to continue.

"Well, uh, I think one of our group did have contact with him. Just before we left."

Vautrin raised an eyebrow. "One of your group?"

Jane nodded.

Vautrin made the rolling motion with his hand again.

Jane cleared her throat, uneasy about implicating Henry McEdwards just because she had seen him hand Hayes something before they left Montgomery. On the other hand, she reasoned, there could be charges of withholding information if she didn't tell.

"One of the men in our group, Henry McEdwards. I saw him hand Paul Hayes something just before we left Montgomery." Jane's voice trembled as she spoke.

Vautrin scribbled something on his notepad, and when he had finished, he put his pen down and gave his desk a forceful pat of his hand. *"Très bien. Merci."* He gave them a smile and stood.

Hillary stood as well. "We can go now?"

"Mais oui!"

"OK, *may we* go now?"

"But of course. And I will go with you." He was ushering them out.

"Oh, that won't be necessary. I can find my way back just fine." Hillary's Southern accent had never been thicker.

"It is *nécessaire,*" Vautrin said. "I must question the others."

"Oh dear!" Hillary said.

At the same time, Jane mumbled an obscenity under her breath.

Vautrin was oblivious to both. He had already opened the front door and was now studying the van suspiciously. "This is your *camion,* uh, van?" he asked.

"Lord, no, it's not mine! I drive a Cadillac. This is just something we rented." Hillary was opening the door to the driver's side.

Vautrin pulled a pad from his back pocket and a pen from his shirt pocket. "You were driving about half an hour ago on the road between Lenoir and the château?"

Hillary looked indignant. "Well, of course. We had to come report the murder, didn't we?"

Vautrin raised his eyes to heaven and said something incomprehensible under his breath, then wrote down the license plate number.

Jane mumbled another obscenity and slid into the passenger seat.

Hillary was getting in on the driver's side. "What did you say?"

Jane let her breath out slowly. "I believe the appropriate word is *merde.*"

"I am so impressed with you, Jane. You know a lot more French than you let on."

Jane ignored her, closed her eyes, and endured the short but harrowing ride back to the château. Vautrin rode his bike ahead of them and turned off at the winery, apparently to check out the body.

When Jane and Hillary got to the front door of the château, Buddy was standing outside the door, looking worried. "Where the hell you been, Miz Ferguson?" he asked, walking to meet them.

"It's a long story, Buddy."

"I didn't even know you was gone until it got to be past time for supper, and then I seen the van was gone. I hope you ain't in trouble."

"I hope not either," Jane said.

"What do you mean by that?" Buddy looked even more worried.

"Nothing, Buddy. Are the girls still with Beau?"

"Ever'body's inside, waitin' for supper. Say, you didn't pick up any beer while you was gone, did you?"

Jane shook her head. "No, I'm afraid not. But I did pick up a policeman."

"Oh shit!" Buddy's glance had moved to Vautrin, who was now walking up behind them. "You got yourself in some trouble, didn't you? I swear, I cain't let you out of my sight for a minute." He grabbed Jane's arm. "Just be cool. I'll take care of this." He hitched up his jeans, and took a step toward Vautrin.

"It's all right, Buddy, you don't have to—"

"How y'all?" Buddy nodded at Vautrin.

"Pardondez moi? Je ne comprend pas."

"You barkin' up the wrong tree, good buddy. Miz Ferguson, she never done it. Whatever it is."

"Ah, Madame Ferguson. *Oui! Oui!*"

"Wee wee?" Buddy gave him a menacing look. "What are you, some kind of per-vert?"

Jane pulled at Buddy's arm. "That's all right, Buddy, Mr. Vautrin is here to ask us all some questions about—well, I'm afraid there's been a murder."

Buddy's face went white. "Murder? Shit, you in more trouble than I thought, Miz Ferguson."

"No, no, Buddy, it's not anything like that. I mean, Hillary and I found the body, we didn't—come on inside, officer; we'll explain everything.

They were just about to go inside when Jane saw Beau

emerging from the shadows as he walked up the lane toward the house.

He hurried to intercept Vautrin before he could enter the house. "I hope to hell I heard right and you're an officer. There's a dead man back there at the winery, and the killer must have broken a window to make his getaway." Beau extended his hand. "Beaumont Jackson, chief of police in Prosper, Alabama." He glanced at Jane. "Thank God you're safe. I've been looking all over for you."

Vautrin shook his hand. "I am pleased to meet you, Chief Jackson. Edward Vautrin, *le préfet de police,* Lenoir, des Bouches-du-Rhône. I am aware of the murder."

Beau's eyes widened. "You are?"

"Madame Ferguson and Madame Scarborough have informed me."

"But how did they know about . . . ?"

Vautrin opened the door and gestured for Beau to enter. "Come inside, Chief Jackson. We must, how do you say? Get in the bottom of this."

As soon as the front door was opened, the faint odor of charred meat accosted their nostrils. "Oh Lord, the beef! I should have taken it out of the oven. It must have continued to cook after I turned the oven off." Hillary hurried away to the back of the house.

"Summons all the others!" Vautrin called after her. "Tell them they must meet me in the room off the great hall."

With her back to him as she continued to hurry away, Hillary waved one of her hands at him in acknowledgment, then she disappeared behind a massive pillar. At just that moment, Sarah and Shakura emerged from around another pillar, giggling and squealing as Sarah pulled Shakura across the polished stone floor while she sat on a large bath towel.

"Mom! Where have you been? We're hungry! Why did you leave two starving children behind?"

Jane turned to Vautrin. "Do the children have to know about this?"

"I'm afraid I must question everyone." Vautrin didn't sound in the least apologetic. He then led everyone to a grouping of chairs in a small room off the great hall. He was, apparently, familiar with the layout of the château. "We will wait here for the others," he said and positioned himself near the doorway so he could watch for them.

"What's going on, Mom?" Sarah was wide-eyed.

"Is he a policeman? Are we in trouble?" Shakura sounded subdued.

"You're not in trouble. Everything will be all right." Jane wasn't at all sure everything *would* be all right, but she felt the need to pull the girls close to her, so she sat on a small love seat with Sarah on one side and Shakura on the other, her arms around each of them. Beau pulled a chair up close.

"Tell me what happened, Jane. Start from the beginning." Beau seemed to have slipped into his professional investigative mode. Buddy pulled a chair up, too, and listened as Jane told the story, starting with the trek to the winery to buy red wine for Hillary's dinner and ending with Vautrin following them back to the château. She tried to keep the details to a minimum in deference to the girls.

Hillary walked into the room with Henry and Lola behind her. "Here we are. You can start now." She glanced at Henry and Lola. "I found these two in the kitchen, cooking eggs and toast." The tone of Hillary's voice sounded as if cooking eggs and toast was as great a crime as murder.

Lola gave her a menacing look. "We had to have *something* to eat. The dinner you said we'd have at six-thirty was ruined."

Henry appeared disgruntled. "What's this about the police here to see us?"

Vautrin stood and introduced himself. "There has been a murder. An American. These two women say they found the corpse."

"Oh my God!" Lola turned suddenly pale and sank down

in one of the chairs. Henry hurried to her side, his hand on her shoulder.

"An American, you say?" Henry asked.

Hillary leaned toward Henry and spoke in a dramatic, hushed voice. "You're not going to believe this, but it was Paul Hayes."

Henry looked stunned. "Paul . . ."

Lola finally managed to speak. "How did this . . ."

"It is my hope that we can put this behind us soon and that your holiday will not be ruined," Vautrin said. "But first, I must ask you some questions."

Henry, Lola, Buddy, and even Sarah and Shakura were questioned as thoroughly as Jane and Hillary had been earlier. When it appeared he was finished, Vautrin looked at Henry and asked pointedly, "Did you have any contact with Monsieur Hayes prior to your departure from the United States?"

"Contact?" Henry looked confused for a moment. "No, I, uh, well, I did see him in the Montgomery airport."

Vautrin nodded. "You spoke to him?"

Henry wiped his face with his hand. "Well, yes, I did. He just happened to mention to me that he was coming to France—"

"Henry!" Lola was looking up at him, still pale, and her eyes wide with alarm.

Henry swallowed hard. "Well, I just said, what a coincidence, so are we, and I gave him a brochure I had in my pocket about this, what do you call it? Château? This place we're staying in."

"Oh my Lord," Lola said, holding her head in one of her hands.

"That is all?" Vautrin asked. "A brochure?"

Henry nodded. "That's all. I swear. Just a brochure."

Vautrin, who had been writing everything on a pad now tapped his pen absently on the paper. "Very well," he said at last. "I must ask all of you to remain in the area for at least a day or two until the investigation is complete."

Jane held her breath while Vautrin pulled another pad from his pocket and wrote something on it. She was certain it was a traffic citation for Hillary, but Vautrin simply flipped the pad closed and replaced it in his pocket.

"Au revoir," he said, moving toward the door.

"Oh, just a minute!" Hillary called to him.

Vautrin turned around, eyebrows raised.

"Have you ever considered brightening up your office a little with curtains and upholstery done in one of those wonderful Provençal prints?" She continued in spite of Vautrin's puzzled frown. "Blue flowers on a yellow background would be nice, and it's neutral, you know, so it would be appropriate for whether the criminal you bring in for questioning is male or female."

Vautrin's puzzled frown only deepened, and then, as if he didn't know what else to do, he gave Hillary a weak smile and a nod and hurried out the door.

"You know where to find me!" Hillary called to his back.

5

Hillary had everyone up by seven the next morning for a Continental breakfast of fresh fruit, strong French coffee with lots of milk, and croissants, which she baked herself.

After breakfast, Henry and Lola planned to view the ruins of an ancient castle while Hillary and Jane went to their first day at the cooking school. Beau promised to take the girls on an outing.

"Want to come along, Buddy?" Shakura asked.

Buddy pushed away the plate of fruit in front of him. "Naw, y'all go on. I'm going to see if I can't find me some ham and eggs." He leaned toward Jane and whispered, "I hope to God they can teach that woman something in that cooking school. She can't cook worth a damn."

Jane gave him a sympathetic look. "I don't think you're going to find ham and eggs here, Buddy. Why don't you just go with Beau and the girls, and—"

"Why, sure, I can find ham and eggs. They's bound to be a truck stop around here someplace." Buddy was already getting up from the table. He pulled his NRA cap down firmly on his forehead and started for the front door. "I'll meet y'all in the van," he said over his shoulder to the group. "You can drop me off in town when you take Henry and Lola in."

Jane glanced at Beau, a worried look. Any time Buddy was on his own, Jane worried. Vautrin was not likely to be sympathetic toward Buddy taking any opportunities to brush up on his "profession" while he was in the village. All they needed to make a bad situation even worse was a burglary rap to go along with the murder that was already complicating their lives.

Beau seemed oblivious to Buddy's movements, however. He was engrossed in telling Sarah and Shakura about wild horses that roamed the marshy delta at the mouth of the Rhône. He had offered to help Vautrin with the investigation any way he could, but Vautrin had assured him everything was under control. Beau seemed more than willing to allow himself to go into full vacation mode.

Hillary, in the meantime, was trying to hurry everyone out so the domestic staff could clean the kitchen and make the beds and so she wouldn't be late for her school.

Within a few minutes, Jane was waving good-bye to Sarah and Shakura as they drove away with the others in the van. She and Hillary set off on the short walk to the cooking school, called L'École de Cuisine Hulot, which sat on a bluff above the river behind the house.

Jane wore jeans, a red T-shirt, and white sneakers. She reached for Hillary's hand to help her up a particularly steep area of the trail, glancing at Hillary's crisp black linen pant suit with a contrasting white collar and black patent pumps.

"I thought Madame Hulot said you were supposed to dress casually," Jane said.

Hillary stooped to brush dust from the top of her pumps. "Jane, dear, this *is* casual dress. People expect more of you when you're—well, when you're not from California."

"I see."

"It doesn't matter what you wear, really, so long as you take accurate notes for me."

"I'll do my best, Hill."

The heavy wooden front doors were wide open, leading into the ancient stone and plaster farmhouse that had been converted into Madame Hulot's school. Jane could see a thin and wiry middle-aged woman buzzing around inside.

She looked up from where she was arranging bowls and platters on a counter as Jane and Hillary entered the building.

"Ah! *Bonjour!* You must be Madame Scarborough. And your assistant? Jane Ferguson? I am so glad you are here!" Her accent was heavy. She walked toward them with an exuberant spring in her step and extended her hand. "I am Madame Hulot. You are the first to come this morning. The others will be here soon."

Madame Hulot led them to a long table and pointed to the chairs around it. "Please, please, sit down. You will have the choice seat. Here, see? Next to my counter where I will show you all my tricks. It is good you have come, you know. I will teach you the best kind of French cooking. It is the *cuisine bourgeoisie*. That is the best, you know. It is the root of all the *grande cuisine*. But better. Ah yes, better. It is what all the tourist like when they go to the little place. You know? They say, oh it was a little place, but the food . . . ah the food! Yes, I will show you all the secrets of a *restaurant de quartier*. Regal, but not expensive. It is the intuition I will teach you. The intuition about how each ingredient will react with other ingredients."

Madame Hulot went on chattering nonstop as the other eight students, British and American, came in and took places at the long table. Madame Hulot explained that this was her English-speaking class and that she hoped each of them spoke English and that she would teach a class for French speakers and one in Spanish later, but she was sorry, she would not teach a class for those who spoke Germany,

because her mother had forbidden her to learn the language
as a young girl.

It was the war, she said, that turned people against Ger-
mans. A very bad thing, the war, she said, and speaking of
bad things, had anyone heard about the dead man in the
wine vault?

There was a murmur in the crowd that seemed to confirm
that at least some had heard about it.

Madame Hulot leaned forward and spoke in a low voice,
as if she was telling a secret. "They say he was murdered
by one of the Knights Templar. Can you imagine such a
thing? They have all been dead six hundred years! But that
is the way things are in this village. Some things never die.
Why, the chapel of the Knights Templar still stands, does
it not? And the symbol of the Knights Templar was on the
man. An American, so they say. And six hundred years?
That is nothing! Not like in America where something is—
what do you call? Antique? In only fifty years? No, we
look at things differently here. Six hundred years is not so
long. Not so long to be dead, certainly. One is dead for a
very long time, after all, and that is the reason we must
enjoy life, n'est-ce pas? And all the more reason to enjoy
good wine and good food, which is what I am going to
teach you . . ."

Madame Hulot went on talking, skipping from one subject to another, but Jane had stopped listening. She was
staring at Hillary, who was staring back, wide-eyed.

Hillary leaned forward and whispered, "My lord! Is she
saying Paul Hayes was murdered by a six-hundred-year-old
man?"

Jane shook her head and whispered back. "I'm not sure
what she's saying. What did she mean by 'the sign of the
Knights Templar'?"

"The mark of civilization! Madame Hulot's voice
boomed, drawing Jane's attention back to her. Madame
stood with her finger pointed to the ceiling, as if to punctuate her point. "Ah yes, any Frenchman will tell you that

to eat well is the mark of civilization! *Mais oui, il faut dîner bien!"* She glanced around the room, pacing back and forth behind her counter with nervous energy. "You, Madame Scarborough." She pointed a finger at Hillary. "Tell me, what is your favorite herb for cooking?"

"Well . . . I declare, I . . . uh." Hillary's face was flushed and her eyes darted about nervously, like a schoolgirl who had been caught passing notes in class. "My favorite herb? Why, I don't think I have one. I mean, it depends . . ."

"Très bien!" Madame gave two quick claps with her hands, cutting Hillary off in mid-sputter. "You are correct, of course. There are no favorites. When you cook something, it must be a blend of ingredients, herbs, spices, whatever, that will tone down a flavor or enhance a flavor in order to create the taste delicious, the dish perfect!"

Hillary pulled out her notepad and shoved it in front of Jane. Hillary sat, completely absorbed throughout the remainder of the lecture and demonstration as Madame Hulot held forth on the right balance of ingredients.

Jane tried to concentrate on taking notes as well, but she found her mind wandering away from parsley and chervil and garlic and thyme. She drew a small sketch of the chapel of Saint Denis in the margin, another sketch of the winery, a rough drawing of a knight in full armor, as well as a note to herself: "Talk to Beau about this."

By the time Madame Hulot declared a break after two hours, served café au lait to the students, and then reconvened for the final two hours of the day, Jane had a disorganized page of notes and a bottom that was numb from sitting.

Hillary, on the other hand, was exhilarated. "It was wonderful, wasn't it? That demonstration on *déglacer* was worth the price of the school. Did you get all of that down in your notes? I'm so glad I have you here. Before I hired you, I had to concentrate on taking notes and couldn't absorb everything."

"Hillary, don't you think we should ask Madame Hulot

what she meant by the sign of the Knights—"

"Did you write down that part about the exact temperature when you're using wine for *déglacer* to keep it from boiling? And I certainly hope you made a note of the length of time to boil sour cream."

"Huh? Oh, yeah. I think I did."

Hillary was still full of enthusiasm as they made their way down the path back to the château. "That's the important thing, you know," she said, picking her way through the shrubs and rocks that interrupted the trail. "The preciseness of temperature, of measurement, of everything! Isn't it wonderful the way she makes you see how the perfect blend can make all the difference? It's like art, you know. Like a Van Gogh painting. Just the right blend of yellow with—"

"Hillary, about the Knights Templar . . ."

Hillary frowned. "The Knights Templar? What do they know about cooking? They're into fund-raisers and old-fashioned uniforms."

Jane stopped, staring at Hillary. "What did you say?"

"I was saying, isn't it wonderful the way Madame Hulot makes a person see the parallels of art in food and—"

"No, about the Knights Templar. Fund-raisers? Old-fashioned uniforms? Hillary, you talk as if they still exist. The knights, I mean. I don't care what Madame Hulot says, six hundred years *is* a long time to be dead."

"Well, they're not all dead, of course," Hilary retorted.

By now they had reached the front door of the château, and Hillary was inserting her key in the lock.

"What do you mean, they're not all dead?" Jane followed Hillary into the château, trying to get her attention. "I don't know about you, but I don't ever see any guys running around Prosper in suits of armor fighting off infidels."

"Well, of course not!" Hillary was still walking ahead of her, headed for the kitchen. "I told you, they're into fund-raisers and marching in parades like the rest of the Masons. I'm going to try out the recipe for tournedos, and if I can perfect it, we'll have it for dinner tonight. I'll make us a quick sandwich for lunch, since everyone else seems to be out still. Cucumber on buttered slices of French bread. Sounds lovely, doesn't it?"

Jane caught up with Hillary at last and forced her to stop and look at her. "Masons? Hillary, what on earth are you talking about?"

"I wasn't talking about Masons. I was talking about cucumber sandwiches."

"No, you said something about the rest of the Masons."

"Oh, you mean the Knights Templar? That's one of the degrees of the lodge. Billy's been one for years. They don't wear armor anymore, but they have black suits with fancy red piping and these cute little hats with feathers on them that make them look like one of the three musketeers, and they have cocktail parties and do good works."

"Did Paul Hayes have the Knights Templar degree?"

Hillary gave her another one of her dismissive waves and started toward the kitchen again. "I don't know. I never kept up with all of that. It's just silly little boy games to me."

"Listen, Hillary . . ." Jane hurried to catch up with her again. "Don't you see the significance of this? Madame Hulot said something about the sign of the Knights Templar being on the body."

Hillary pulled out a skillet. "Jane, honey, she was talking about the *dead* Knights Templar. The ones who used to terrorize the country. Only don't tell Billy that, for heaven's sake. He prefers revisionist history. He doesn't want to hear that they ever did anything bad. Hand me the butter from the fridge, please. Smell it first, to make sure it's fresh. It should be. I ordered it this morning."

Jane opened the refrigerator, but instead of searching for the butter, she was still looking at Hillary. "How do you know she was talking about the dead Knights Templar?"

"Well, she had to be, didn't she? What would she know about Billy's lodge in Prosper?"

"The sign, Hillary. What's the sign, or the symbol, of the Knights Templar?"

"Are you going to hand me the butter? And make sure there's fresh sour cream in there, too, oh, and mushrooms. I think it's called a Maltese cross. Do they look fresh?"

"I don't know what a fresh mushroom looks like, but here they are. Here's the cream. It's OK, I guess, and the butter just smells like butter." Jane handed it to Hillary and peered deeper into the refrigerator. "What's that other stuff you want? Malted what?"

"Maltese cross. The symbol of the Knights Templar, and I think a slice of foie gras on each tournedo would be perfect. Could you pick me up some in the village later? It's red, and they have it on their sleeve."

"I thought it was sort of brown."

"No, it's red."

"Who has it on their sleeve?"

"The Knights Templar."

"Foie gras on their sleeve?"

"No, lamb, the cross. The Maltese cross. And on banners, too, I think.

"Oh! The Maltese cross!" Jane rubbed her temples, which were beginning to throb. "Did Paul Hayes have it on his sleeve?"

"I doubt it. He probably didn't even know what foie gras is."

"Oh, there you are!" Sarah burst into the kitchen, followed by Beau and Shakura. "We had a great time, Mom. I wish you could have been with us! Beau took us to a place called the Camargue, and there were wild white horses running on the beaches."

"And flamingoes," Shakura added. "Real live pink ones. They were everywhere, and we saw a wedding in the town with everybody on white horses."

"Even the bride!" Sarah said, breathless with excitement. "And we found a McDonald's, and Beau bought us lunch!"

Hillary sucked in her breath and crossed her rose-tipped

hands over her heart, then gave Beau a look as if he'd taught the children to use an off-color word.

Beau shrugged and feigned an innocent look. "At least we had *French* fries."

Hillary turned quickly toward Jane. "Potatoes, of course! Madame Hulot said potatoes would not detract from the tournedos. You must pick up some for me when you get the foie gras."

"Tornado?" Shakura's eyes were wide. "Here? Do we have a storm cellar?"

"No," Jane said. "In France, a tournedo is something you eat."

"Wow!" Shakura said. "Wait till Buddy hears that."

Sarah giggled, and Beau turned to Jane. "I'll take you into the village. Buy you some lunch if you haven't eaten."

"Oh please, do go, lamb," Hillary said. "I do want to get started experimenting, and we can have those cucumber sandwiches another time."

"Well, Ok." Jane did her best not to appear too eager to comply. She glanced at Sarah and Shakura. "Get in the car, girls. You can come along, too."

Sarah immediately protested. "Oh, Mom, do we have to? Can't we stay here and work on the model horse kit Beau bought us?"

"Well . . ."

"Mrs. Scarborough will be here to watch us," Shakura said, obviously trying to be helpful.

Jane raised a cautionary eyebrow, but Hillary placed her hands on Jane's shoulders and turned her around, directing her toward the door. "Go on, lamb. I'll watch the girls. Have lunch if you want, but don't forget. Foie gras and *pommes de terre.* I'm sure you know that means potatoes. Madame Hulot told us that today, and it must be in your notes."

"Please let us stay! Please!" Shakura and Sarah pleaded together.

Beau already had Jane halfway to the door. "They'll be all right," he said.

Still, Jane hesitated. "Well, OK, but stay in your room. Don't go outdoors alone. Don't bother Mrs. Scarborough. Make sure you—"

"They'll be all right," Beau said again, his hand on her elbow in a firm grip.

Jane wasn't so sure. There was a murderer loose somewhere, and Hillary Scarborough, who had never had children of her own and who sometimes needed taking care of herself, might not be the best choice as a baby-sitter.

By the time they'd made the short drive into the village and located Le Monastere, a restaurant in a hotel that had once been a medieval monastery, Jane was beginning to relax.

After she'd had half a glass of wine, she felt even more relaxed, and she'd stopped telling Beau how uncertain she was about leaving the girls with Hillary. She was working now on getting the mental picture of Paul Hayes dead in a vat of wine out of her mind. She had told Beau the rumor Madame Hulot had passed along about the sign of the Knights Templar.

Beau refilled her glass with the deep red table wine the waiter had brought while they waited for their meal. "Don't worry about it, hon. That cop. What's his name? Edward Vautrin? He seems capable of taking care of it. And I wouldn't pay any attention to rumors. You always get 'em when something like this happens."

Jane ran her finger around the rim of her glass, toying with it, the way she was toying with that image in her mind. She had even forgotten to protest when Beau called her *hon*.

"Well, I didn't like the way he questioned Hillary and me. I mean, it sounded like he thought we did it," Jane said.

"Standard procedure." Beau sounded very relaxed. "He was just doing his job. I would have done the same thing."

He chuckled softly. "Just glad it's his responsibility and not mine. This is the first vacation I've had in five years, and I'd forgotten how nice they are."

Jane gave him a smile. "I'm sorry. I'll try to stop talking shop to you."

"Hey, I like that smile. You know how long I've waited to get you alone like this? And this is perfect. Good wine." He raised his glass. "Great atmosphere." He glanced around at the ancient trees and rows of begonias and petunias in the enclosed garden where they sat. "And a beautiful woman."

Jane blushed. She'd never been called beautiful before.

"So, will you let the police worry about the murder and just enjoy it here?" Beau said.

Jane felt a pleasant warmth moving through her like a lazy, tropical river. "I'll do my best."

"Good. Then there's nothing that can spoil this moment."

"Hey there, Miz Ferguson, I thought I might find y'all here. I got some good news!" It was Buddy, walking toward them from the garden entrance. He was carrying a large grocery sack.

After a pause that Jane knew might have lasted slightly too long, she said, "Hello, Buddy. Won't you, uh, join us?"

Buddy had already seated himself next to Jane and across from Beau. "You was right, Miz Ferguson. They ain't a café in this whole town that even knows what ham and eggs is. But the good news is, they got grocery stores, just like we do at home, and I bought us some." He rattled the sack. "Sure was hard to find beer. All they wanted to sell me is wine."

"Is that *all* you did this morning, Buddy?" Jane gave him a suspicious look.

"No, ma'am, I spent my time looking around and learning things."

Jane raised a nervous eyebrow and glanced quickly at Beau and then back to Buddy. "Learning things?"

"Yeah, I was just walking around, you know. Amongst

all them houses that's kind of like apartments on them little
ol' narrow streets, and—you ain't going to believe this—I
come up on that cop that was out at our place last night.
And he has all these other cops with him, see, and they
was talking in that funny language, you know, that don't
sound nothing like American—"

"French, Buddy. That's the native tongue in France."

"Whatever. Anyhow, even if I didn't understand his talk,
it wasn't too hard to figure out that he was talking about a
break-in at this one house, and I just stood back and
watched until I figured out how the guy done it."

Beau frowned and nodded his head knowingly. "You at-
tended a friggin' seminar on how to break into a three-
hundred-year-old house."

Buddy looked hurt. "I never said that." He glanced at
Jane. "I never said nothing like that, did I, Miz Ferguson?"

Jane reached to pat his hand. "Everything's all right,
Buddy. Let's just make sure it stays that way."

Before Buddy could reply, they were interrupted by another voice booming a greeting.

"Ah, Madame Ferguson, Monsieurs Jackson *et* Fletcher,
bonjour, bonjour! I am so glad I have found you!"

Jane glanced up at the greeter. "Monsieur Daudet!"

"Join us," Beau said, with a flat note of resignation in
his voice. He pointed to a chair.

Daudet sat down, shaking his head. "Oh, it is horrible!
A dead man in my wine vault, and what is worse, my guests
are the ones who found him."

"Vautrin—the policeman—he must have told you that
Hillary and I were the ones who—"

"Ah, yes, he told me everything." Daudet looked as if
he might weep. "I don't know how it could have happened!
I don't know that man or how he got into my winery. How
did the intruder get past the locked door when I am the
only one with the key? How is it that the dead American—
what was his name? Hayes? How is it that he was inside?

The one who killed him, why did he choose the Mas du Compte for this terrible crime?"

"I'm sure the police will get to the bottom of this," Beau said. He looked very much as if he wished he were someplace else. Or at least that Daudet and Buddy were someplace else.

"I, uh, I heard something today, Mr. Daudet." Jane shifted uneasily in her chair. "A rumor. About the corpse, I mean—"

"Ah yes," Daudet interrupted her. "Inside his coat was a handkerchief embroidered with the sign of the Templars."

Buddy sat up straighter. "Come again? He had what in his coat?"

"You didn't mention this," Beau said. The look he gave Jane was part accusative, part worried.

"Well, I . . ."

Buddy looked confused. "What the hell's a Templar?"

"They were knights, Buddy," Jane said. "You know, knights with shinning armor. You've heard of that."

"Oh yeah, like the ones y'all said built that little ol' chapel we was in like a hundred years ago or something."

"Seven hundred," Daudet said. "The order has been around for eight hundred years. It started in the north of France. They were knights who escorted pilgrims to the Holy Land and their home was a building they believed to be the temple of Solomon."

"That's the stuff that was in that brochure about the château," Beau said. "The guy that built it was one of the knights."

Daudet nodded. "*Oui*. He left the order because he did not want to give up half his holdings as the Templars required of him. Some say that is good. Some say the Templars became too powerful. They were Europe's bankers, you know. After the infidels forced them out of Jerusalem. Very powerful. Special dispensations from the church. I'm afraid some of them became rogues. Especially after power was wrested from them by King Philip and the Inquisition."

Jane frowned, trying to understand. "But the handker-chief with the sign? What does that mean?"

"Ah, the cross. So confusing. Now it is the Maltese cross. First it was the Latin cross. The Maltese cross belonged to another order of knights who took over the property of the Templars, and then the Freemasons, well, they confused matters even more by rewriting history to reflect their origins in the Templars and claiming the Maltese cross." Daudet shook his head. "I don't know. It is so confusing."

Buddy was pouring himself another glass of wine. "What the hell does all this have to do with that ol' boy that died?" He set the bottle down hard.

Daudet dismissed Buddy's question with a shake of his head. "A rumor. Only a rumor that the ancient Templars are responsible for the murder."

"Oh hello!" Lola called as she and Henry advanced toward the table. "We've been walking around the castle and the village and the river for hours, and thought we'd have some lunch. Mind if we join you?"

"The more the merrier." Beau had a wry tone to his voice.

Buddy chugged his wine down in one long gulp. "We was just talking about that dead man."

"Oh dear!" Lola looked stricken. Henry was looking at Daudet and wearing a puzzled frown.

"You haven't met Mr. Daudet, have you?" Jane said. "He owns the winery where the, umm, where Mr. Hayes was found." By now the salad she'd ordered for lunch had arrived, and she was trying to eat it.

"Oh, I see." Lola turned pale, as if the reminder of Paul Hayes's body was unsettling to her.

"Well, I'll swear," Henry said, still frowning.

"I was thinking of taking the train to Avignon tomorrow while you and Hillary are in class," Lola said, intent upon changing the subject. She looked around the table. "Anyone want to go with me? I'm not sure Henry wants to go."

"Depends," Buddy said.

"I think I'll wait for Jane," Beau said.

Buddy gave Beau a cautionary look. "You go on, if you want to. I'll see after her."

Jane made her own quick attempt at changing the subject. "Mr. Daudet was just telling us about the Knights Templar."

Buddy poured another glass of wine. "There's a rumor that they done it. Them knights, I mean."

"Really?" Lola poured herself a glass.

"The knights?" Henry looked puzzled.

"Never mind," Jane said. "I think I can see a logical explanation."

"She's real smart," Buddy offered to anyone who was listening.

"A logical explanation. As to why the poor man was killed?" Lola asked.

"Well, not exactly," Jane admitted. "But there's a possibility he was a member of the order of Knights Templar in the Masonic lodge and maybe he just happened to have a handkerchief in his pocket with the emblem on it. It wasn't necessarily put there by whoever strangled him."

"Strangled?" Beau, Lola, and Henry asked at once.

Jane felt embarrassed. She hadn't meant to go out on a limb with so little information. "Well, he *looked* strangled. I mean there didn't appear to be any bullet wounds or anything, and there was that deep purple spot on his neck."

"That could have been the wine staining his skin," Beau said.

Jane nodded and tried to brush away her silly mistake with a wave of both hands. "I know, I know. Just a guess. He could have been poisoned. Who knows."

"Poisoned? Of course. We will check for that in the autopsy." This time it was Vautrin who joined the table, pulling up a chair without waiting to be asked.

"How's the investigation coming along?" Beau asked.

"It is progressing," Vautrin said vaguely. He glanced at Buddy. "Did I see you in the village today?"

"Yeah. I was out lookin' for beer."

Vautrin raised his eyebrows. "Beer? Ah, but while you are here, you must enjoy our wine. Or pastis, the native liqueur."

"But of course," Daudet agreed and began a long discourse on the virtues of wine, and of the wine of his vineyards in particular. Buddy had at last succeeded where others had failed. He had changed the subject.

It was, as it turned out, a pleasant enough gathering and relaxed conversation over lunch and wine. When Jane and Beau started back to the château, Henry, Lola, and Buddy were in the van with them. It was only at the last minute that Jane remembered to buy the foie gras and potatoes Hillary had wanted.

Hillary met them at the front door. "Jane! I must talk to you. In private."

"If it's about the notes I took—"

"I couldn't make heads or tails of anything, Jane. I haven't even started the *tournedos avec crème.*" Hillary was literally wringing her well-manicured hands.

"Excuse me, guys," Jane said over her shoulder to Beau and Buddy. She knew when it was time to soothe the boss. Behind Hillary, Jane could see Sarah and Shakura seated next to one of the pillars, executing an elaborate hand slapping and clapping ritual while chanting a rhyme. They gave Jane only a cursory glance by way of greeting.

Jane led Hillary into the kitchen, away from the others. "Look, Hill, I'm sorry about the notes. I promise to do better next time. It's just that I was so preoccupied with—"

"Oh my Lord, lamb, it's not the notes. You always write in hieroglyphics. I'm getting used to it. It's this." She handed Jane a slip of paper. "It came just minutes ago. There was a knock at the front door, and since the staff is gone, I answered it myself. This note must have been stuck in the door, because it fell on the steps as soon as I opened the door.

Jane opened the paper. It was plain white paper with an

oily stain around the edges. In the middle was a cross crudely drawn with a red pen. Beneath it were the words, *"Prends garde!"*

"I don't know what it means," Hillary said, "but it must be something dreadful. It's written in blood!"

It took Jane several minutes with her French-to-English dictionary and the companion reference book on irregular verbs to determine that the meaning was quite simply "Beware!"

6

Dinner was going to be late.

Hillary was edgy. "Jane, what does this mean? 'Add butter and cook until dead in a wine vat?' " She shoved the notes under Jane's nose.

Jane looked at the notes. She was edgy, too. "How do I know what it means, Hillary? You were there. Don't you remember what she said?"

"You were supposed to be taking notes."

"There weren't supposed to be any dead men to distract me."

Hillary banged a heavy frying pan down on a gas burner and squinted at the notes again. "And this: 'Scrape bottom of pan with Henry and Paul Hayes'?" She turned to Jane, an annoyed frown creasing her forehead. "Jane what is this?"

Jane looked at the notes again and pointed a finger at the sentence Hillary had just tried to read. "That doesn't say scrape the pan with Henry and Paul Hayes. That's a new sentence. See, it says here, 'Scrape the pan until' . . . something. And the new sentence is, 'Check with Henry *about*

Paul Hayes.' " She stabbed at the paper with her finger as if to emphasize that it made perfect sense.

Hillary shook her head. "Henry McEdwards and Paul Hayes have nothing to do with *tournedos avec crème*. I have to figure out this recipe, Jane. Madame Hulot said we had to practice tonight and bring a sample to class." Hillery sighed and paced the floor. "I was depending on you, and you let me down. You've got to stop being hysterical."

"I'm hysterical? How about you when we found the body, and then that note in the door . . ." Jane took a deep breath and sat down in one of the chairs in the kitchen. "OK, Hill, you're right. Maybe I am hysterical. But I've got my ten-year-old daughter and her best friend with me in a foreign country where someone has just been murdered. That's all I could think about while we were in that cooking class. I'd cut my right arm off before I'd let anyone hurt either of those girls."

Hillary turned the heat off under the tournedos she'd been sautéing in butter and sat down next to Jane. She looked tired and worried. "I know, lamb. I'm sorry I was cross. I'm worried, too. What are we going to do?"

"The smart thing to do is let the police handle it," Jane said.

Hillary nodded. "You're right." She glanced at Jane and a smile flirted at her lips. "But maybe we could help solve the mystery. We're getting pretty good at it, you know."

"No, Hillary."

"You know you're dying to dig into this."

"Don't use that word, Hill."

"So where do we start?"

Jane gave her a warning look. "We start by showing that note to Beau and then going to the police and keeping our noses out of it."

Hillary stood up and went back to the skillet. "You're right. We'll keep our noses out of it."

"Hillary . . ." There was a warning in Jane's tone.

"What?" Hillary had a wide-eyed, innocent look.

"Don't—"

Hillary held up her hands in a gesture of surrender. "I'm keeping my nose out of it."

"No you're not. You gave up too easily."

"Don't be so suspicious, Jane. I'm sure I'll be too busy with my cooking classes to think about it anymore."

"Mom! Come listen to this new rhyme we made up!" Sarah's voice called from another part of the house.

Jane hesitated a moment, still wondering what Hillary might have in mind, but she gave in, finally, to Sarah's insistent call.

Dinner, though late, was delicious. Even Buddy was pleased.

"Dang, Miz Scarborough, this tastes nearly as good as one of them steak sandwiches you get at Shoney's," he said between mouthfuls.

Everyone except Hillary and Beau scraped away the foie gras, and Sarah picked off all of the mushrooms, but the dinner was still proclaimed a success by all. Hillary was beaming, and Jane had stopped worrying about Hillary trying out her detective skills.

It had been such a perfect meal that Jane was almost reluctant to show Beau the warning note Hillary had found. She knew she was going to have a difficult time telling him about it without upsetting the other guests. Finally, though, after the meal was over and the girls had gone to play with their model horse and the others were engaged in an argument about whether credit cards or traveler's checks provided a better rate of exchange, Jane managed to whisper to Beau.

"Can you meet me in my room after the girls have gone to bed?"

The spoon Beau had been using to stir his coffee clattered against the saucer when he dropped it, then fell to the floor. Beau turned a surprised stare toward Jane, and everyone else turned to stare at Beau.

Jane realized her poor choice of words too late. "Oh no, I didn't mean—"

"Well, yeah, I mean, I guess, I mean yeah!" Beau said at the same time Jane was speaking.

"Was the coffee too hot, Beau?" Hillary gave Beau a solicitous look.

"No!" Beau said quickly. "It was, uh, it was . . . I mean yes, the coffee's hot. Just right hot. Not too . . . I'll just get my spoon now." He ducked down suddenly as if he might be trying to hide from the others.

"What'd you do, goose him?" Buddy asked Jane. He was scooping his seventh spoonful of sugar into his coffee.

Jane's only reply was a weak smile.

"What are everyone's plans for tomorrow?" Hillary was either oblivious to the awkward situation at hand or else she was making a gracious attempt to alleviate it.

"I thought we'd take the train into Avignon," Lola said. "Maybe walk through the old Pope's Palace and do some shopping."

Henry shook his head. "You go ahead, pet. After walking all day today, I'd like to stay around here and rest."

"And you, Buddy?" Hillary asked.

Buddy shrugged. "Hang out with Beau and the girls, I reckon. At least till Miz Ferguson's free."

"Oh yes," Hillary said. "I'm sure there are plenty of places to take the girls. Maybe those old ruins nearby. What are they called? Les Baux, I think. Why, I'll bet a person could stay there all day."

It was only then that Jane realized what Hillary was doing. She was trying to make sure everyone was occupied and out of the way so she could indulge herself with her snooping and detective work. Jane tried to give her a warning look, but Hillary was now occupying herself with telling Henry that a trip to Avignon with his wife would be a lovely adventure.

When the meal finally ended, everyone gathered in one of the sitting rooms while the staff cleared the table and cleaned the kitchen. Jane hoped for an opportunity to explain to Beau what she'd meant by asking him to her room, but the opportunity never came, thanks to Buddy's close scrutiny and the need to make sure Sarah and Shakura went to bed at an early hour.

Jane had just tucked both the girls in when a soft knock came at the door. She was expecting Beau.

"Hillary!" she said when she opened the door.

Hillary stepped into the room quickly, her eyes wide. "I've got to talk to you, Jane." She glanced around the room at the clutter of clothes hanging on a chair, cosmetics strewn on the dresser. "My, my," she said under her breath.

"Is something wrong?"

"I'm not sure." Hillary stepped over a bath towel Jane had let fall to the floor and sank to the bed, crumpling something in her hand, and Jane could see that she was shaking.

"Something *is* wrong Hillary. What is it?"

Hillary took a shuddering breath. "Someone has been in my room."

"I hope someone has been in your room. This place is costing us enough, the maid should be in at least once a day."

"No, I was still in my room this morning when Eugenie came to clean. She only stayed a few minutes. Whoever it was came later."

"Eugenie?"

"The maid. She told me that is her name."

"All right," Jane said, trying to be patient. "How do you know someone came in later?"

"Because I found this." She thrust the crumpled paper toward Jane, and when Jane unfolded it, she saw a crude cross drawn with the same red pen in which the warning note had been written and on the same type of paper, oil-stained around the edges. Jane felt her body grow cold, as if her blood had stopped circulating.

"This was in your room?"

Hillary nodded.

"And it wasn't there when you went up to freshen up before dinner?"

Hillary shook her head.

"Then that means someone was in there just before dinner."

Hillary gave Jane a frightened stare.

"But who? Henry? Lola? Beau? One of the girls?" Jane asked.

"Nobody has a key to my room. Except that girl, Eugenie, and I don't think she has been back." Hillary crumpled the paper again. "This is scary, Jane. We've got to find out who's doing this."

Jane shook her head. "No we don't. We're going to leave it to the police. We'll tell—"

Before she could finish her sentence, she heard another knock at her door. She walked quickly to the door and opened it to see Beau standing in front of her.

"Jane, I hope you meant it when you said for me to come—Hillary!" He glanced at Hillary and then back at Jane, wearing a confused look.

Jane stepped aside. "Come in, Beau. There's something we want to show you." She gave him both notes. "See those French words, *'Prends garde!'* That means beware. I looked it up."

"So?" Beau handed the papers back to her, obviously unimpressed.

"Don't you see the connection?" Jane pointed to the other one. "A cross. The sign of the Templars. Just like they found on Paul Hayes, and—"

Beau's chuckle sounded a little strained. "You're getting upset over nothing, Jane. You're smart enough to know that the handkerchief Hayes had stuffed in his pocket was his own, with an emblem from his lodge."

"Maybe so, but why is someone painting crosses on paper and writing threatening words?" Jane said.

Beau shook his head, maybe a little condescendingly, Jane thought. "Probably just a joke."

Hillary stood up from where she'd been sitting on the bed. A jerky, nervous movement. "But I found the second note in my room. That's no joke."

"Could be a joke," Beau said. "Could be the girls put it there. They're both pretty precocious, you know. They can probably figure out how to write a two-word warning in French."

"But they wouldn't do that!" Jane sounded more than a little defensive. "They wouldn't purposely try to frighten Hillary."

Beau frowned. "Sorry, hon."

Jane always had the urge to warn him not to call her hon, but then she also always had to take stock of the fact that Beau was Southern, not chauvinist. "Just to make sure, I'll ask the girls if they did it," Jane said. "In fact, I think we should ask everyone in the house what they know about this. Then I think we should turn it over to the police."

Beau smiled. "Good idea. We'll assemble everyone in the parlor and question them while we watch their faces for signs of deception."

He'd gone over the line. "Don't patronize me, Beau."

Beau held up his hands as if to ward off her anger. "OK, OK, I'm sorry. It's just that I think this has more of the trappings of a practical joke than anything sinister, and I think that French policeman will probably see it the same way, but if it makes you feel better—"

"It will certainly make *me* feel better," Hillary said. "I don't like the idea of someone being in my room. Why, what if they come back while I'm in there? Oh, I wish Billy would hurry and get here!"

"If it will make you feel better, ma'am, I'll switch rooms with you," Beau said. There was, Jane thought, something to be said for the Southern gentleman, chauvinist or not. "Then if whoever put the note in there comes back, you won't have to worry," Beau added.

Hillary's face brightened momentarily, then she appeared hesitant. "Well . . ."

Jane gave her a concerned look. "What is it, Hillary?"

"It's just that the masculine look isn't my style, and those dark, earthy tones don't go with anything I brought."

"Are you crazy?" Jane's tone was impatient.

"One should always decorate to suit one's personality and chose colors that will complement the physical appearance of the individual." Hillary spoke with utter confidence.

"What?" Beau looked confused again, but Jane only chuckled.

"Stick to your guns, Hillary." Jane spoke, not without cynicism. "You'd die before you'd stay in a room that didn't measure up."

Hillary's eyes widened. "Well, since you put it that way . . ."

Beau turned back to the door. "OK, it's settled, then. We'll switch rooms; but first, just to make you feel more comfortable, I'll question the others."

"I'll go with you," Jane said, "and I'll get the girls. I don't think they're asleep yet." She had left open the door to the bathroom, which separated her room from Sarah and Shakura's room, and she thought she could hear them giggling.

In a little while everyone was assembled in one of the sitting rooms downstairs.

"What's this all about? I was sound asleep, and I need my rest if I'm going to walk all over Avignon tomorrow." Lola, her hair wound up in pink foam-rubber curlers, made no attempt to hide the fact that she was disgruntled.

Henry merely seemed groggy and had very little to say. Buddy, who, doubtless, had been questioned many times before by the likes of Beau Jackson, was suspicious. "What you calling us all together for? Something's going on, ain't it? I ain't done nothin', I'll guarantee you that."

Shakura and Sarah were wide-eyed and curious and obviously happy for any excuse not to have to be in bed.

"This won't take long. Just a question or two I want to ask all of you." Beau had taken on his professional stance, standing in the middle of the room with the others seated around him. "Seems we may have a practical joker around somewhere. Trouble is, it's not a very funny joke. It's got Hillary and Jane upset, and when that happens, it ceases to be funny."

He showed everyone the two papers and explained the circumstances under which each had been found. Lola gave them a cursory glance, scowled at nothing in particular, and readjusted one of her curlers.

The sight of the two papers seemed to bring Henry awake at last. He stared at them and mouthed, "Good Lord! What a stupid, terrible thing to do."

Buddy seemed relieved. "Is that all you called us down here for? Just them little ol' papers? Hell, that ain't nothin'. What's that word mean, anyhow? It ain't nothing porny-graphic is it? 'Cause if it is, I'll have to get Miz Ferguson and Sarah out of here. Ol' Jim Ed would want—"

"Relax, Buddy." Jane patted his hand. She was beginning to feel embarrassed and was starting to think that Beau was right. It was probably just someone's idea of a practical joke. Probably had nothing at all to do with the murder.

Beau turned to Sarah and Shakura. "You girls know anything about this?"

They both shook their heads with solemn expressions. Sarah edged a little closer to Jane. "What does that mean, Mommy? Does it mean something bad?"

Jane put her arm around her daughter. "Maybe it's just a joke, like Beau said." She placed her hands on Sarah's shoulders and turned her around to face her. "You didn't go in Mrs. Scarborough's room did you?"

Sarah looked surprised. "Go in her room? Of course not." Her voice quivered, as if she might cry.

"No, we didn't. Honest, Mrs. Ferguson." Shakura's voice had the same tearful quiver.

Beau squatted to be on the girls' level. "It's OK," he said. "I believe you. This is just somebody's bad joke. Don't worry. We'll get to the bottom of this."

"You believe us? We're not in trouble?" Shakura still looked shaken.

"You're not in trouble, and of course I believe you. You wouldn't lie to Uncle Beau, would you?" Both of the girls shook their heads, and Beau gave Shakura a quick hug and Sarah an affectionate chuck of her chin. "OK, back to bed, both of you. We've got lots of stuff to do tomorrow."

Jane watched Sarah and Shakura scramble away. Her anger toward Beau was beginning to cool.

Beau stood and spoke to the adults. "OK, everybody else can go back to bed. I know we're all a little edgy because of what happened to Paul Hayes, but I don't think there's any reason to be scared. Just to make sure, though, I'll show these papers to that cop, what's his name? Vautrin? I'll do it tomorrow before I take the girls off to Les Baux. The rest of you go ahead and have fun and forget about it."

Henry and Lola started back to their rooms, with Lola grumbling about needing her rest.

Buddy called to Jane as she walked away. "Want me to come check your room, Miz Ferguson? Make sure there ain't no Frenchy in there playing practical jokes?"

"Thanks just the same, Buddy, but I'm sure everything's all right." Jane didn't dare tell him that Beau would be next door in case any problem did arise.

"I'll help you move your stuff," Beau said, walking toward the stairs with Hillary.

Jane followed with the girls. When she had once again put them to bed, she went through the bathroom, to her own room. An eerie feeling overtook her as she stepped into the room. She wasn't certain what it was, but it crept down her spine and she froze near the bathroom doorway, afraid to advance farther into the room.

She tried to shake off the feeling and took another step

into the room. Someone had been in there. She sensed it without knowing just how. And then she saw that the large white Turkish towel she had left crumpled on the floor was not there, the same towel Hillary had stepped over when she came in.

Jane whirled around and saw that someone had hung it on the towel rack. Someone who had been in the room while she was downstairs with the others.

7

Jane's first reaction was to rush through the bathroom to the room where Sarah and Shakura slept to make sure they were safe. She opened the door quickly, too nervous to be quiet. She almost cried with relief when she saw them, each curled up in her twin bed.

She crept into the room, wanting to kiss Sarah on the forehead in gratitude for her safety, but as she started toward the bed, a noise behind her startled her. It was coming from her room, and it sounded as if someone was still in there.

For one moment she stood dead still, listening. She heard it again: a rustling or perhaps a scuffing of feet. Quickly, she whirled around, just in time to see, through the space of the bathroom that connected the two rooms, the blur of a figure rushing toward the door leading from her room into the hall.

Jane hurried through the bathroom. "Who's there?" she called. Just as she reached her room, the door leading to the hallway closed. Jane sprinted across the room, jerked the door open, and saw someone in the shadowy hall running toward the stairway. There was no mistaking that the figure was a woman, in spite of the fact that she wore jeans and a T-shirt. When she turned in profile to start down the stairs, Jane recognized Eugenie, the girl who cleaned the rooms.

"Eugenie! Stop!" The girl ignored her and raced down the stairs. "Stop!" Jane was now standing at the top of the stairwell. "What were you doing in my room?"

Jane was about to start down the stairs after her when she heard a door open behind her and Beau's voice calling, "What's going on?"

Jane glanced over her shoulder. "It's Eugenie. That girl who cleans the rooms. I caught her in my room snooping around!"

Beau hurried to join Jane on the stairwell. "Did she take anything?"

"I don't know, but she's about to get away."

Beau moved past her and bounded down the stairs, calling out in his policeman's voice, "Stop! Right where you are!"

The girl ignored him and kept running through the great hall and out the door, with Beau running after her and Jane behind Beau.

"Damn!" Beau stood just outside the door, staring into the darkness. The girl had disappeared into the thickness of the night. Beau turned to Jane. "She's gone." He shook his head.

"What's going on? What was all that racket I heard?" Buddy was skipping down the stairs in his bare feet and his shirt open, revealing a large Confederate flag tattooed on his almost hairless chest.

"It's OK, Buddy. I just thought I heard something, that's all," Jane said.

"You heard something?" This time it was Hillary coming down the stairs behind Buddy. "Was it whoever was in my room?"

"Jane heard someone in her room just now," Beau said. "One of the cleaning staff."

"In Miz Ferguson's room?" Buddy looked alarmed, and Jane was wishing Beau had kept his mouth shut. She didn't need anything to encourage Buddy's overly protective nature. "Damn! I guess I better plan on sleeping out in the hall tonight in case you need me."

"Oh no, Buddy, I'll be fine. You don't have to—"

"It's OK. I'll be sleeping in the room next to her." Beau's words brought a scowl to Buddy's face.

"Do what?" Buddy glanced at Jane. "If ol' Jim Ed knew about this . . ."

"Oh Lord, none of us is safe!" Hillary was pacing the floor in her feathery high-heeled mules. "It won't do me any good to trade rooms with Beau."

Jane tried to comfort her. An overly protective Buddy and a hysterical Hillary was certainly more than she needed. "I'm sure there's no danger, Hillary. It was just Eugenie. She was probably just looking for something to steal."

"Who's looking for something to steal?" This time it was Henry at the top of the stairs, dressed in a red velour bathrobe with his yellow pajama legs showing at the bottom. Lola was behind him, wearing a lurid peignoir in a shade of red that clashed with Henry's bathrobe and with the pink rollers that still lurked like rows of tainted sausages in her hair.

Beau stepped away from the door. "I think everyone should go back to bed. There's nothing we can do about this now. I'll talk to that cop in the morning."

"Talk to the cop about what?" Henry had come farther down the stairs.

"Someone was in Jane's room. We think it was the girl who cleans the rooms. Probably looking for something to steal." Beau sounded like the take-charge policeman he was back home in Prosper.

"Good Lord, the staff stealing from us?" Henry started down the stairs in an angry flurry. "We ought to lodge a complaint with the manager. We ought to sue, by God!"

Lola stayed at the top of the stairs, scowling.

"Mom? Why is everybody downstairs?" Sarah and Shakura were winding their way around Lola.

"The noise woke us up," Shakura said. Both girls looked sleepy and a little frightened.

"It's OK. Nothing to worry about." Jane had started toward the girls. "Just go back to bed. Come on, I'll go with you."

"You sure you don't want me to sleep in front of your door?"

"I'm sure, Buddy." Jane flung the words over her shoulder.

Henry turned around to go back to his room. "I think we should, by God, sue!"

"Stupid girl!" Lola said, following behind him. "You just can't get good help anymore."

When they were upstairs, Beau stopped in front of the door to his room. "I'll be right next door. Just call out if you need me."

Jane gave him a quick smile and a wave as she walked behind the girls into her room. It was only then that she realized that Hillary was behind her. She followed Jane into the room and closed the door.

"Hillary . . ."

Hillary adjusted the sleeve of her brocade dressing gown. "Put the children to bed, lamb, then we'll talk."

"Talk about what?" Sarah asked. "About the maid? Do you think she knows something about the dead man? Can we listen, too? Please, Mom!"

"Absolutely not!" Jane pushed the girls toward their room and gave Hillary a warning look. "And there's no reason for you to think the maid had anything to do with anything other than snooping around my room. I don't know where you get ideas like that."

"Mom!" Sarah stood, facing Jane, with her arms akimbo. "Don't you see that all of this has to be connected somehow? The dead man, the scary notes, somebody snooping around?" Shakura, standing next to Sarah, nodded her head in agreement.

"No, I don't see, and anyway, don't you two have better things to think about?"

"Geez, Mom, you treat us like children!"

Another gentle shove. "You *are* children, sweetheart, and I want both of you in bed."

Jane tucked the girls in once again with the unmistakable feeling that there was going to be a lot of whispering going on between them after she left. She turned around just before she left the room. "Go to sleep now." The girls were already pretending sleep, a sure sign, she knew, that she'd spoken impotent words.

Hillary was thumbing through a translation of Balzac Jane had brought with her to read and had left by her bedside. She put it down as soon as she saw Jane—a quick gesture, as if she hadn't really been looking at the pages anyway. "Did you really mean what you told the girls? That you don't think any of this stuff is connected?"

"I don't know, Hillary." Jane sank down heavily on the bed and leaned her head against the headboard. "It's just that I don't want those two children's minds filled with thoughts about murder. They should be thinking about horses in the Camargue and whether or not American French fries are better than French French fries. Shakura's mom would have her home on the next plane if she knew what was going on."

"You think they're right, don't you?" Hillary was frowning and tapping one of her enameled nails on the arm of the chair. "That it's all connected, I mean."

Jane nodded. "Could be. There's some logic to it. First the hint that there's some connection to Paul Hayes's death and the Templars, then those weird papers showing up with what could be the sign of the Templars on them, making us think someone's been in your room when they shouldn't be. Then the maid showing up in my room when she shouldn't be."

"Well, I didn't have it all figured out so logically. I just feel it here." Hillary put her hand on her stomach. "Deep inside me, I just know there is some connection, and, Jane, you have to put a stop to all of this. It's ruining everyone's vacation, and I'll never be able to put together one of these tours again if this gets out. Besides, I need to concentrate on learning the techniques Madame Hulot is teaching. I simply don't have time for murder!"

"Well, geez, Hill, I don't think the murderer realized how put upon you would be; otherwise, he might not have done it." Jane got up and started for the bathroom to get into her robe.

"This is not the time to be cynical, Jane."

"What was it you wanted to talk to me about?" Jane called out to Hillary from the bathroom as quietly as possible, trying not to disturb the girls.

"I want you to do something about this."

Jane came out of the bathroom, toothbrush in hand. "And what do you propose that I do?"

Hillary gave her an incongruous look. "Well, how should I know? I was brought up to be a lady."

"What's that supposed to mean?"

"Oh, I'll help you, of course. I told you earlier, I'm getting pretty good at this detective work, but you have to get things started."

Jane shook her head. "I told you, the only thing I think we should do is go to the police."

"But the police aren't doing anything, lamb. And I'm having trouble concentrating on my class."

Jane pointed her toothbrush at Hillary. "Look at it this way, Hillary, if you get too involved with the detective work, you won't have *time* to concentrate on your cooking class. You don't have time for murder, remember?"

"Well that's just the point. We have to get it solved so I can get back to concentrating, and if you'd like, I can show you a wonderful way to organize your closet."

"Organize my what?" Hillary's nonsequiturs had a way of keeping Jane off balance.

"Your closet, lamb. I have a wonderful technique. It works well whether you've just unpacked your clothes for a stay in a hotel or your closet at home." Hillary was scrutinizing Jane's closet and the haphazard way she'd hung her clothes and left part of her suitcase unpacked and sitting on the closet floor.

"My closet? Oh yes, good. Just what I need." Anything, Jane thought, to get Hillary's mind off of playing detective.

"We'll do it later. After we've solved the murder."

"Hillary . . ."

"Come on, Jane. You know you're itching to get into this. Why, you've already come up with that wonderful logical explanation. We're halfway there. We'll have this solved in a snap. Before it ruins everyone's vacation and therefore my reputation, and I can use my full mental powers concentrating on—"

"Hillary . . ."

"You are, aren't you?"

"I'm what?" Jane tried to busy herself fluffing her pillows.

"Itching to get into this." Hillary pointed a pink-tipped finger knowingly at Jane.

"No."

"Who do you think did it?

"I don't know, and I'm not going to—"

"I know who did it."

"Hillary, I'm not going to get into this with you. We are going to keep our noses out of it, and what do you mean you know who did it?"

"Eugenie and that winery owner. What's his name? DooDah."

"Daudet."

"You're coming along *so* well with your French, Jane." Jane threw her pillow aside and put her hands on her

hips in a gesture of impatience. "Hillary, where did you get
the idea that Eugenie and Daudet are the murderers?"

"Well, it's not all that hard to figure out, is it? She's
snooping around our rooms, so that has to mean she's into
it somehow. But she wouldn't be strong enough to put Paul
Hayes in a wine vat, would she? I mean, she hardly weighs
a hundred pounds. So she had to have an accomplice. Who
was in the winery just before poor Paul was discovered?
No one but Daydaw."

"Daudet."

"Whatever."

Jane sat down on the edge of the bed, thinking she had
cause to worry about herself when Hillary's explanations
started seeming logical.

"But what about a motive?" Jane said finally.

Hillary gave her one of her feathery waves. "Oh, I don't
know, I haven't gotten that far yet, but it will come to me."

"Oh Lord!" Jane said.

"I can see the wheels turning." Hillary pointed a finger
at Jane. "You're thinking about it, aren't you?"

"No, I'm not thinking about it," Jane lied.

Hillary's eyes were wide with enthusiasm. "Here's what
I think we should do. Tomorrow after class, we'll take another walk down to the winery. Pretend we want another
tour of the place. And you'll engage, what's his name?
Daudet? In a clever conversation, and he won't suspect
you're fishing for a motive."

Would that work? Jane wondered. Was it even a reason-
able thing to do? After all, Guillaume Daudet certainly
hadn't given any reason to make anyone suspect him during
the relaxed conversation she and Beau had had with him at
the restaurant earlier. But then, he could have been cleverly
hiding something, couldn't he? It was, after all, certainly
curious that the dead man had been found in Daudet's wine
vat.

Jane realized that she had hesitated too long before answering when she heard Hillary speak again. "I can *hear*

those wheels turning. OK, here's what we'll do. As soon as class is over, we'll dash over there, and you'll ask all the clever questions, then afterward, I'll come home to start dinner. We're going to start with a wonderful salad with endive and flat-leaf parsley and mint leaves. It will all be delivered in the morning, along with some loaves of French bread. We can pick up a nice red wine while we're at the winery."

"Hillary, wait a minute!" Jane called to her as Hillary started for the door. "You're acting as if we're going to have this whole thing solved by noon. We can't—"

"Oops!" Hillary had opened the door and stumbled over Buddy, who was curled up in a makeshift bedroll in front of Jane's door. "See you in the morning, lamb," Hillary said over her shoulder. "I've got to get to bed now. If I don't get enough rest, I get bags and circles."

Jane looked down at Buddy, started to wake him up, but instead shook her head and closed the door. She dropped onto her bed and picked up the Balzac novel Hillary had been leafing through, but she could only look at the words without comprehending.

She was reluctant to admit it, but she really would like to question Daudet a little more. He claimed not to know Paul Hayes at all and to have no idea why he would be found dead in his winery. Was Hillary right? Was he the most likely person to have been at the winery when Paul Hayes died? He had, however, told everyone there that evening that, as soon as they left, he was closing for the day.

If the door wasn't locked as it should have been when she and Hillary went back later, who unlocked it? Daudet said he was the only person with a key. Was he lying? Or had someone stolen one? Or did he unlock the door himself?

Who was the shadowy figure she and Hillary had seen in the winery after they found the body? Daudet or an interloper?

OK, she thought, Hillary was right. She *was* itching to

get to the bottom of this. She'd wanted to question Daudet further when he'd joined her and Beau at the restaurant, but as more and more people joined them at their table, she'd become reluctant to probe. But if she and Hillary could see him in private and engage him in conversation, would they be able to get some answers?

What could it hurt to try? She turned out the lamp next to her bed and fell asleep to the sound of Buddy snoring outside her door.

The next morning, Jane once again had trouble concentrating on the notes Hillary had her taking while Madame Hulot expounded on the proper way to cut fish for bouillabaisse.

She was thinking, instead, of the events of the night before and wondering just how they should approach Daudet to get him to talk freely.

Sarah and Shakura were on her mind as well. She'd left them with Buddy with strict instructions that they were not to leave the château until she returned. She'd promised to go with them to the ruins at Les Baux in the afternoon.

Lola had gotten up early to get the train to Avignon while Henry slept in. Beau had left after breakfast to fill in the policeman, Vautrin, on the events of the night before.

Jane tried hard to stop thinking about what the others were doing, and what Sarah and Shakura were doing in particular, and to listen to Madame Hulot instead.

By the time she'd watched Madame Hulot and Hillary wack off the heads of several varieties of fish and scoop out their entrails, she was feeling queasy. Then she had to smell the fish boiling in a pot of water with spices—such a long list of spices she wasn't sure she'd gotten them all down correctly for Hillary.

When the class was over and Madame Hulot served her creation as lunch, Jane had lost her appetite completely.

"Well, that was enlightening, wasn't it?" Hillary said as they made their way down the hill again. "Cooking the filets only half as long as you cook the remaining fish seems to make a difference. I've never done it that way, have you?"

"Never," said Jane, who had never heard of bouillabaisse until she met Hillary.

"I think tomorrow we're going to do coquille Saint-Jacques."

"I can hardly wait."

Hillary studied her face. "You look a little green, Jane. Are you all right?"

"Just don't talk about fish anymore."

"Don't you like fish, Jane?"

"Not after today."

They had reached the château by now, and Hillary rushed off to wash the fishy smell from her hands while Jane checked on Sarah and Shakura. She found them in the garden playing with a jump rope while Buddy watched over them with the protective attitude of a guard dog. He had even made them a lunch of peanut butter and jelly sandwiches on leftover French bread, using the peanut butter and jelly Jane had brought with her. Jane had brought it along, knowing the culinary tastes of ten-year-olds would not run to haute cuisine.

"Oh dear!" Hillary looked moderately shocked when she saw the sandwiches. "You should have used the avocados. They make wonderful sandwiches when you mix them with a little gourmet mustard and dill, maybe a little chervil and tarragon. And freshly squeezed lemon juice, of course."

"That don't sound like it would taste good with peanut butter," Buddy said.

"Can we go see the ruins now?" Sarah asked.

"They say there's a real catapult there that they used to throw stones at the Saracens," Shakura said.

"Throw stones?" Buddy gave Jane a worried look. "Ain't that kind of violent for a little girl? Maybe we ought to take them someplace else."

"I think it will be just fine, Buddy, and the history lesson will be good for them," Jane said, wondering why she had ever worried about leaving the girls with Buddy. She turned to the girls. "We'll go as soon as Mrs. Scarborough and I get back. We're going to take a short walk down to the winery to talk to Mr. Daudet. Go upstairs and get your cameras and plenty of sunscreen. We'll only be a few minutes."

Jane was wondering again how she had let herself get into snooping around with Hillary as they walked to the winery.

"There's no guarantee that we're going to learn anything, Hillary," Jane said. "And we're not going to spend a lot of time snooping around. To be honest, I just can't imagine that nice Guillaume Daudet had anything to do with the murder."

"Why, Jane Ferguson! You're loosing your nerve. This is not like you." Hillary was walking briskly in the gold lamé tennis shoes she changed into, along with black designer jeans and lots of gold jewelry.

Jane kicked at a pebble with her sturdy Nikes. "I'm not losing my nerve, Hillary, just coming to my senses. I don't know why I let you talk me into such a foolish thing last night. You caught me in a weak moment."

"Don't think of this as foolish, Jane. We've got to get this taken care of as quickly as possible for our own good."

"Oh yeah. You don't have time for murder, and besides, it's not good for business."

Hillary stopped and put her hands on her hips. "How do you always end up making me sound so materialistic and foolish?"

Jane saw the hurt look on Hillary's face. "Oh geez, Hillary, can't you see it's just that I'm edgy about this? We could end up just like Paul Hayes, you know."

Hillary's eyes widened and she turned suddenly pale. "But why would anyone want to put *me* in a wine vat?"

"Because you've learned something that's dangerous for you to know." Jane pushed open the door to the winery.

There were two people inside, a woman checking labels on bottles and a man, dressed in work clothes, attending the wine vats.

"Oh dear," Hillary said. "Now that you put it that way . . ."

"*Bonjour,*" the woman checking the labels said.

"*Bonjour,*" Jane replied. "Is Monsieur Daudet in?"

The woman shook her head. "*Je ne parle pas anglais.*"

Hillary leaned toward Jane. "What did she say?"

"I don't know, but I think that means he's not here."

"You're just making that up because you've lost your nerve."

"Haven't you?"

Hillary's eyes went to the wine vat where Paul Hayes had once floated. "Well . . ."

"*Merci! Merci!*" Jane said, smiling and backing away. "Let's go home and forget about this," she said to Hillary when they were outside.

"Maybe he's in the chapel," Hillary said. "Look, the door's open."

Jane glanced at the chapel, then back at Hillary. "OK," she said with a shrug. "We've come this far. Let's go have a look. But if he's not there, we're not pursuing this any further."

"You know, I've been thinking about that chapel," Hillary said as they walked up the rocky path to the entrance. "It's terribly small, but it could be made to look larger if the walls were painted a lighter color and some of those icons were removed."

"Hillary, you don't redecorate a medieval chapel, I don't care *how* good your design sense is."

Hillary ignored her. "I did one of my TV shows on that—how to make a room appear larger. I wonder if there's some way to break into French television. I'm sure there are a lot of people who would be interested."

Jane pushed open the door to the chapel and stepped inside. She froze as soon as she saw the altar.

"You could make this high ceiling work to your advantage if you . . . Good Lord, Jane, that's Eugenie up there on that altar." Hillary's voice had dropped to a whisper. "And that's Henry lying on top of her! Can you believe it? In a church!" She nudged Jane. "Now's your chance. Go ask her if she stole anything from your room. Go on, you won't be embarrassed. You're from California.

Jane found it difficult to speak. "I can't, Hillary," she finally managed to say. "They're dead. I can't ask them anything."

8

"Dead? No, they can't be. That's impossible. I know a compromising position when I see one." Hillary leaned closer to have a better look at the two.

"They're dead, Hillary. Those blue gray faces. Those marks on their necks. You can see them even from here. Just like Paul Hayes." Jane felt as if the cold, stone walls of the tiny chapel were closing in on her.

"Oh no, Jane, I can't take much more of this. This is three bodies we've found. You know I don't like dead bodies." Hillary was backing her way out of the chapel.

"I'm not any more fond of them than you are, Hill."

Hillary grabbed Jane's hand. "Come on, let's get out of here. Let someone else find the bodies."

Jane allowed Hillary to pull her outside the chapel, but she stopped in front of the door. "We can't do that, Hillary. We have an obligation to go to the police."

"Are you sure about that, Jane? After all, you only have a couple semesters of law school, and anyway, the laws may be different in France." There was a frightened urgency to Hillary's voice.

"Not that different. We have to go to the police." Jane emphasized each word.

"Oh, all right, then. You go and tell them what you found. I'm going back and soak in the tub with cucumber slices on my eyes to try to get rid of these bags I got from you keeping me up so late last night." Hillary had already started to walk away.

"Come back here, Hillary!" Jane called. "You can forget about your cucumbers. You're in this as deep as I am."

Hillary turned around to face Jane. "But you're the one with the law degree. You know what to say."

"Oh, so now I have a law degree. A moment ago it was only two semesters." Jane shook her head. "You have a way of manipulating words to suit your purpose. Anyway, we would never have found the bodies at all if you hadn't insisted we start snooping around."

"So now it's *my* fault, is it?"

"It's certainly not *my* fault," Jane said.

Jane and Hillary glared at each other, and Jane thought she saw Hillary's chin quiver as if she was about to cry. "Oh listen to us, Hill, we sound like a couple of ten-year-olds. Worse. I've never heard Sarah and Shakura do this. We're both just upset, that's all."

"What are we going to do?" Hillary said as she reached to embrace Jane in a hug.

Jane returned the hug, then held her at arms' length. "We have to go to the police, Hill. We have to tell them what we found."

Hillary shook her head, more in despair than in disagreement. "I just can't believe this. Why would Henry be with that woman? And think of his wife! Poor Lola. She has absolutely no taste in clothes, and her house is done in that tacky Spanish Colonial motif, but I wouldn't have wished *this* on her! You just never know about people, do you? I mean, who would have thought Henry would be caught dead philandering."

"I don't think he was philandering, Hillary." Jane was leading Hillary back to the house.

"Talk about sacrilege! Henry even went to a Catholic high school."

"Someone killed them and just dumped them there."

Hillary stopped and stared at Jane, speechless for a moment. "How do you know that?" she asked finally, in a weak voice.

"Well, I don't know anything for sure, of course. But it doesn't take a medical investigator to tell those two people were strangled. Just like Paul Hayes. My guess is they were killed someplace else and dumped in that chapel because somebody was in a hurry to get them out of sight. Maybe whoever did it was going to come back for the bodies later or something."

"But why?" Hillary shook her head as if she didn't want to believe any of it.

"I don't know why," Jane said. "Why was Paul Hayes killed? Why all those cryptic messages about the Knights Templar? Why was Eugenie in our rooms? Was she the one who put the messages in there? Is her death connected to that somehow? Is Henry's death connected because he knew Paul? Will one of us be next because we knew Henry?"

"You're scaring me, Jane."

"It is scary. And that's why we've got to go to the police. We'll take the van into the village and do it right away. Then one of us has to tell Lola her husband is dead when she returns tonight. I'm certainly not looking forward to that."

"Jane, do you really think it's necessary for me to talk to that policeman? Do you? I mean I don't speak French, and I wouldn't know what to say even if I did. You're the lawyer, after all, and you were married to Jim Ed Ferguson for almost ten years."

"What does that unfortunate incident have to do with it?"

"Well, he was a criminal lawyer when you were married

to him, wasn't he? I mean before he started representing all those stuffy insurance companies."

"I'm not following your logic, Hillary, and I don't speak French either, which doesn't matter since Vautrin speaks English."

"But you're so much more clever with that sort of thing than I am, and some of Jim Ed's skills must have rubbed off on you. I'm just a housewife. Although I *am* quite good at culinary skills and interior design and gardening, and I do have one of the most popular TV shows in Prosper, I am still, just a lowly little—"

"Give it up, Hillary."

"You have to do this for me, Jane."

"Why are you so afraid to talk to that policeman?"

"He doesn't like me. He thinks I purposely tried to run him down when he should know perfectly well that he was taking up too much of the road. And anyway, it's what I pay you to do."

"There's nothing in my contract about talking to the police."

"Well, of course not. I don't even *think* about things like that. I'm a law-abiding citizen."

"Except for traffic laws."

"What!" Hillary sounded incensed, but in the next second her mind had flitted elsewhere. "Why, Beau Jackson, there you are!" Hillary waved to Beau, who had just driven up in the van as they approached the driveway leading up to the château. "We'll tell Beau everything," Hillary said to Jane while she continued to wave and smile. "I'm sure he'll agree that I have nothing to do with this whole thing."

"Jane? Are you all right?" Beau was getting out of the van as Jane and Hillary approached.

Jane had an urge to reach out to Beau to steady herself. Someone to lean on. Instead, she crossed her arms tight around her torso. "We've just found Henry. Dead. And—"

"Oh God!" Beau shook his head, as if he were shaking

away trouble. "I was hoping they'd secure the crime scene before anyone—"

Jane was puzzled. "Secure the crime scene? You mean the police know already?"

Beau nodded, then looked distracted. "Someone's got to tell Lola about Henry when she gets back from Avignon."

"You know, maybe it wasn't a crime at all. It could have been a heart attack." There was a hopeful ring to Hillary's voice. "Sometimes that happens, you know, an older man with a young woman. In a compromising position. Did Vautrin think of that?"

Beau now looked confused. "What?"

"It wasn't a heart attack, and it wasn't a compromising position. It's Henry and Eugenie, and they're dead! In the chapel!" Jane, still with her arms wrapped around her torso, was beginning to sound hysterical, even to her own ears.

"Oh, hon!" Beau reached for her and encircled her in his arms. Jane was caught off guard. If they had been back home in Prosper, Beau would have maintained a professional attitude, taken out his notepad, and begun asking questions. For a second, she let herself relax and buried her face in his shoulder. He pulled her closer for just one brief moment, then gently pushed her out at arm's length from him. "What were you doing in the chapel?"

"We'd been to the winery to find Mr. Daudet," Hillary said, answering for her. "He wasn't there, and when we left, we saw the door to the chapel open, so we peeked inside, and that's when . . . Well, Jane knows the rest."

"We saw them, the two bodies, on the altar. And I knew they were dead. They looked like they might have been strangled."

A flicker of emotion flared in Beau's eyes, but it was quickly extinguished by the professional armor he donned from habit. "Why were you going to see Daudet?" he asked.

"Well," Hillary said, "we were going to—"

"Chat!" Jane said before Hillary could reveal too much.

"We were just going to chat." Jane knew Beau would not approve of their probing.

"Uh-huh." Beau eyed them both with a look of suspicion. "Well, if you want to chat with Mr. Daudet, you'll have to go down to the local jail."

"The jail?" Hillary asked.

"What do you mean?" Jane asked at the same time.

"Guillaume Daudet has just been arrested for the murder of Paul Hayes. And Henry and that young woman."

"Oh!" Hillary said.

Jane could only look at him with a shocked expression.

Hillary turned to Jane with a smug look. "Didn't I tell you? I said he was the one who did it, didn't I, Jane?"

Jane nodded. "You did, Hillary. You did say that."

"I want to have a look at the bodies," Beau said. He had assumed his professional demeanor. "Then we'll talk to Vautrin."

"We?" Hillary said.

Beau nodded. "He'll want to question both of you."

"Oh dear," Hillary said.

"But why?" Jane asked. "If he had already found the bodies . . ."

"He'll want to know what you were doing there." Beau had already started walking toward the chapel, and Jane had to run to catch up.

"When was Daudet arrested?" she asked.

"Early this morning sometime. They were already questioning him when I got there."

"Well, if Daudet was being questioned at the police station, then he couldn't have killed these two, could he?"

Beau stopped his hurried walk long enough to look at Jane. "That depends. We don't know what time these two were killed."

Beau came out of the chapel looking grim. "Looks like you're right, Jane. It appears they've been strangled. There are some funny looking smudges on their clothing, too.

They'll need lab tests, of course, but my guess is it's grape stains. Or wine."

Hillary nudged Jane. "You mean like someone who had been working with grapes did it? Someone like Daudet?"

Beau didn't answer. He had already started walking back to the château. "On second thought, I think it's best if you two don't go into the village with me. Wait at the château, because I'm sure Vautrin is going to want to come out again for more investigation."

It wasn't easy for Jane to explain to Sarah and Shakura that two more bodies had been found, and that they wouldn't be going to see Les Baux that afternoon. In the end, although they left the room somber and subdued, they took it better than Buddy.

"Miz Ferguson, I got to get you and Sarah home on the next flight!" Buddy was pacing the floor, looking agitated. "It's plain as day they got something against people from Prosper over here."

Jane did her best to calm him. "I can see why you might draw that conclusion, Buddy, but I don't think being from Prosper has anything to do with it. That young woman, Eugenie, wasn't from Prosper."

"And what about a motive?" Jane asked. She had to hurry, because Beau was on the move again. "He claimed he didn't even know Paul Hayes. Why would he want to kill him? And he'd only met Henry briefly. Why would he want to kill *him?*" Jane was asking all the questions she'd wanted to ask Daudet.

"I don't know what the motive was," Beau said. "But he could be lying about not knowing Paul and Henry."

"But why would he lie?" Jane insisted, still playing devil's advocate.

Beau shook his head. "I don't know. And I don't know why he might have killed that girl."

"But you've got to be curious," Jane said. "Two people from Prosper killed here in France? Why?"

By now they had reached the door of the chapel, and Beau didn't answer Jane. Instead, he stepped with caution into the chapel. "You two wait out here. No point in contaminating the scene any more than is necessary." He flung the words over his shoulder as he entered the building.

"And to think we were all in the winery with the murderer that night. Why, he could have killed us all! He doesn't seem to need a motive," Hillary whispered when Beau was inside.

"Don't think about it, Hillary."

"You don't think he did it, do you?"

"I don't know what to think."

"Well, I'm just glad he's behind bars. We can all rest easier now."

Hillary spoke up with a bright tone of voice. "But there is a connection! I mean, if she was . . . You know, involved in a little hanky-panky with Henry."

"She was?" Buddy looked surprised. "Well, hell, maybe his wife killed both of 'em."

Jane shook her head. "No, no, no! There's nothing to suggest there was anything between the two, and besides—"

"They *were* lying together on that altar," Hillary said, interrupting.

"They was?" Buddy's eyes were wide. "You mean, like . . ." He wiggled his eyebrows.

Hillary rolled her eyes and nodded her head affirmatively.

"You're jumping to conclusions, Hillary." There was desperation in Jane's voice. "I think they were lying there together because the killer put them there. Just like someone put Paul Hayes in the wine vat."

"Well, I guess Lola was pretty pissed if she just throwed both of them up on that altar." Buddy frowned, deep in thought. "Wonder what she was pissed at Paul Hayes for, though."

"It certainly shouldn't matter to her if *he* was sleeping

with Eugenie." Jane made no attempt to keep the sarcasm out of her voice.

Buddy was wide-eyed again. "He was?"

"No, Buddy, I didn't mean—"

"Not unless Lola was sleeping with Paul Hayes," Hillary said.

"Well, damn, this sounds like one o' them soap operas. Ever'body sleeping around like that!" Buddy looked worried. "This ain't no place for Jim Ed's little girl."

"Will you two stop it!" Jane let her frustration boil over. "This is nothing more than gossip. Unsubstantiated gossip. We have no reason to believe anybody was sleeping with anybody, and even if they were, Lola didn't do it. She's been in Avignon all day."

"Well, then I was right the first time." Hillary sounded smug. "It was Daudet."

"That feller that runs the brewery?" Buddy looked surprised.

"Winery," Jane said.

"He was sleeping with Lola?"

Hillary sucked in her breath in shock. "Oh my Lord, He was? How did you find that out?"

"You just said—"

"You're both giving me a headache," Jane said, putting her head in her hands. "Just listen to me! Nobody was sleeping with anybody! And we're not going to talk about this anymore. We're just going to wait for the police to come and question us again, and for Christ's sake, don't repeat anything you just said. It's all gossip anyway."

Hillary had another worried frown on her face. "Well, if he asks us . . ."

"Just answer the questions, and don't offer any opinions."

"Right," Hillary said.

"Sure," Buddy said, and then added, "Just goes to show, you don't never know what goes on behind closed doors, do you?"

Hillary shook her head. "Who would have thought?"

Jane closed her eyes, and wished for Vautrin.

When Vautrin arrived with Beau, he was as grim-faced as ever. He had already seen the bodies and had other policemen in the chapel checking and securing the scene. Beau had also told him that Lola would be returning on the late-afternoon train from Avignon.

The questioning was routine and very similar to the way they had been questioned after the first murder. Jane was relieved that the only question put to Buddy was about whether he had left the house that morning. His answer had been a simple "No." Buddy was obviously accustomed to giving the police as little information as possible.

Hillary, however, was a bit more talkative. "I can't tell you how shocked I was to see them there like that, and really, who would blame Lola for a crime of passion if *she* had seen them."

"Lola? You mean Madame McEdwards?" Vautrin asked. Jane felt a knot in her stomach tighten and wished she could tighten something around Hillary's mouth. Vautrin continued. "You said, crime of passion?"

"Well . . ." Hillary looked uncertain.

Vautrin leaned toward Hillary, his expression intense. "You are saying Madame McEdwards had a motive?"

Hillary gave Jane a quick, nervous glance. "Of course not. I've said all along I thought it was that Mr. Doodah."

"Doodah?"

"She means Daudet," Jane said, feeling more and more uneasy.

"But what about Madame McEdwards?" Vautrin pressed Hillary. "Of what crime were you speaking?"

"She didn't mean crime exactly, she meant—"

Vautrin interrupted Jane by raising his hand as a signal for her to stop speaking. His focus was on Hillary.

She hesitated for one nervous moment. "Well, of course

I didn't mean crime. What I meant was *if* she had seen them in a compromising position, which it certainly looked like they were in, then she *might* be upset, but I certainly never said she committed a *crime* did I?"

"What is this 'compromising position'?" Vautrin asked, looking confused.

Hillary squirmed in her seat. "Well . . . Tell him, Jane."

Jane did her best to look innocent and confused. "I'm sure I don't know what you're talking about, Hillary."

Beau looked at Hillary, wearing a frown. "You think Henry and that young woman were sleeping together? Is that what you're saying? And that Lola might have . . . ?"

Vautrin laughed then, interrupting Beau. "Ah yes, sleeping together. I understand sleeping together. But no," he said, shaking his head, "sleeping together is not the motive, I'm afraid."

"It's not?" Hillary looked both relieved and confused.

"No, you see, I believe we have the murderer behind bars already, and his motive was more, umm, how do you say? Complicated."

"Daudet?" Jane asked.

"Mais bien sûr."

"But if he was arrested this morning for the murder of Paul Hayes, then how could he have murdered two more people while he was in jail?"

"Madame, Monsieur Daudet was not arrested until almost noon. We have reason to believe we arrested him soon after he committed the second and third murders." Vautrin's words sounded a bit condescending to Jane.

"But what . . ." Jane was about to ask Vautrin what Daudet's motive could be, but a discreetly raised finger and the look on Beau's face stopped her in mid-sentence. His signal obviously meant that she was asking too many questions.

"Thank you for your cooperation," Vautrin said, standing and looking down his long nose at everyone. "I hope you will enjoy the rest of your stay in Lenoir. Please feel confident that we have caught the killer, and that you will have no more problems." He glanced at Beau. "You are meeting Madame McEdwards at the station?"

Beau told him that he was.

"I will be there also, to give her the bad news." He glanced at Hillary. "Perhaps you would like to accompany us as well? To give her comfort?"

"Why of course I will be glad to help," Hillary gushed.

Vautrin was about to leave when he turned back to Jane. "Madame Ferguson, isn't it?"

Jane nodded.

"Ah yes, Ferguson. The name is familiar. You are perhaps related to Jim Ed Ferguson?" He had pronounced it Jeem Ed.

"Why you askin' ?" Buddy broke his silence, speaking up before Jane could deny she was related.

"I visited in Atlanta once about a year ago. Monsieur Ferguson was in the same hotel at a convention. I met him at the bar. He showed me how Americans . . . how do you call it? Become raisers of hell?"

"Oh yeah, I'll bet he did," Jane said.

"You know him then?" Vautrin asked.

"Never heard of him."

9

"I don't understand," Jane said, as she waited on the platform with Hillary and Beau for the train from Avignon. "What possible motive could Daudet have for killing anyone?"

"Meth lab," Beau said. Jane noticed that he had what she had come to think of as his "professional frown" on his face. He was glancing around the station. Probably watching for Vautrin, who was supposed to arrive soon.

"Meth lab? Are you saying Daudet had a meth lab?" Jane felt both alarmed and confused.

"What's a meth lab?" Hillary was repairing her makeup. She had to look her best, she said, to give poor Lola the comfort she would need. She seemed to have forgotten that a few hours earlier she was busy concocting a motive for Lola to murder her husband.

"A meth lab is a home lab for making methamphetamines. You know, speed." Beau glanced anxiously at the tracks in the direction of Avignon.

Hillary sucked in her breath and put the rosy tips of her fingers to her mouth. "Oh my Lord!"

"Vautrin says he found it in the back of the winery. Says he thinks Paul Hayes must have stumbled upon it, too, and that's what got him killed," Beau said, still wearing his frown.

Jane shook her head. "Daudet? No, I can't believe . . ."

Beau shrugged. "He denied it, of course."

"Well, we certainly didn't see anything like that." Hillary glanced at Jane. "We didn't did, we? I mean, I'm not sure I would know what a meth lab looks like."

Jane shook her head. "No, of course not, but I suppose this must mean Henry and that maid did."

"So they *were* together. I knew it!" Hillary said.

"Henry could have gone down to the winery while he was out walking this morning." Beau seemed to be speaking more to himself than to anyone else. "But the maid? I don't know. Why would she have . . . ?"

"She was mixed up in it. I'm sure of it." Hillary pointed an assertive finger at no one in particular. "She was the one who was putting those awful notes all over the house."

"Hillary, we don't know that to be an absolute fact," Jane said.

Hillary looked indignant. "Well, who else could it be? She's the one you saw leaving your room."

"Well, there's that," Jane said. "But what does that have to do with a meth lab?"

Hillary fluttered her fingers in a dismissive wave. "Oh, they'll figure it out. The important thing is, the crime is solved." She winked at Jane. "And we didn't have to get involved. But poor Lola," she said, a shroud of sadness coming down on her face. "Such a tragedy. My, my!"

Jane sighed and shook her head. "Something doesn't seem right. I mean, Daudet doesn't seem like the type to be into drugs or to kill someone."

Beau didn't respond. He was staring at the tracks again, still frowning, still, apparently, thinking thoughts he wasn't expressing.

"You don't think he did it either, do you?" Jane said.

Beau glanced at Jane. "Doesn't matter what I think. Vautrin's the policeman. Over here, I'm just a tourist."

"Did you actually see the meth lab?" Jane was still pressing him, unwilling to give up on it just yet. She was speaking over the sound of a loudspeaker blaring an announcement in French.

Beau nodded. "I was at the station when they brought the equipment in as evidence. And one of those employees we saw when we had the tour came in to make a statement. I wasn't allowed to hear the questioning, and I couldn't have understood anything if I had, but Vautrin told me the guy said he had been helping Daudet make the drug." The roar and whoosh of an incoming train almost drowned out his words.

"Well, my Lord," Hillary exclaimed. She glanced at Jane. "I'm beginning to think it's a good thing we never got to launch our investigation." The train, pulling into the station, was slowing to a stop.

"What investigation?" Beau looked both alarmed and suspicious. All around him, people were moving toward the doors leading to the terminal building.

"Oh look! There's Lola!" Hillary said, and Jane was glad for the excuse not to have to explain anything to Beau.

Lola stopped walking and stared at the three of them as soon as she saw them, as if she knew something was amiss. Beau moved ahead of Jane and Hillary and took Lola's arm, leading her away, and then it was he who told her the news. Lola cried out as if she had been wounded. Hillary took her hand and gushed comforting words to her while Jane stood by, feeling awkward. She was, she realized, nowhere near as practiced as Hillary in such matters. It seemed to be a gift bestowed more generously upon Southern women.

While Beau was explaining to Lola that Henry's body had been sent to Avignon, Vautrin arrived. He went immediately to Lola and explained to her the complicated procedure required to complete the investigation and to ship the body back to Alabama. Lola, who had regained some equanimity, insisted that she would return with the body to Prosper. She said she would stay in Avignon, where Henry's body had been taken, until all arrangements could be made. Beau would arrange to have the bags she and Henry had left at the chateau sent to her.

"One of us will stay with you, lamb," Hillary said. "I know you'll need the support."

"Oh, no, you mustn't," Lola said with a wave of her handkerchief. "Really, the most comforting thing for me would be to know you're enjoying that school. After all," she said with a tearful smile, "I would like to think some good had come of this vacation in spite of everything."

Hillary left her with the assurance that they would pray for her and that she must contact them immediately, through Vautrin, if she needed anything at all.

"Oh, I will, hon," Lola said. "I *know* I can count on you, and I just appreciate it so much. I just hope you understand that I need to grieve alone."

"Well, of course, lamb, but I'm going to worry about you."

Lola shook her head and blinked as if she was blinking back tears, then put a hand to her trembling mouth.

Hillary reached a hand to her again. "Oh, you will get through this, and you will be a stronger woman for it. I just know it. And you have to believe, lamb, that Henry has gone on to a better place."

Lola nodded. "Oh yes, yes, you are so right, darlin'. I know he would want me to be strong."

They went on for a few moments more, exchanging platitudes that were a part of the Southern ritual. Then there was another hug and mutual kiss on the cheek and the ritual was ended. Hillary turned away from Lola, wiping from her eye a tear that had not disturbed her carefully applied makeup in the least.

The mood was heavy and somber as Jane, Hillary, and Beau drove back to Lenoir. Beau dropped Jane and Hillary off in front of the château and drove around to the back to park the van. Hillary and Jane were walking up the short path to the front of the château just as Madame Hulot came pedaling up on a bicycle.

"*Mon dieu!* I have heard the news." She stopped her bicycle and got off. "One of your group has been . . . Oh, it is so *horrible*," she said, leaving off the *h* sound as the French do. "And that poor child, Eugenie. She was even employed by me once. I had to let her go, of course. That type is not suitable for . . . Oh, but I never would have wished such a fate upon anyone. It is too horrible. And the men. The ones who died. You knew both of them, *n'est-ce pas?* Such a tragedy! I have canceled tomorrow's class, of course. Out of respect, you know. But you must not think that this is—how do you say? Typical? Of our village. We are not murderers. And to think of three in one week! *Mon dieu!* There is someone crazy here, *n'est-ce pas?* It is all too, too frightening. But Monsieur Vautrin, we trust him to find the guilty ones. He is new to Lenoir, of course. Swiss!" She said with a slight curl of her upper lip. "There are only twenty years that he has been here. But we must trust, nevertheless."

Madame Hulot's soliloquy might have gone on longer had she not paused to exclaim, "*Mon dieu!*" again and to draw in her breath, which gave Jane a chance to speak.

"The girl, Eugenie, you say she worked for you?"

Madame Hulot nodded. "*Oui,* but only briefly. She helped me clean after my classes, but she was not reliable. She was even at one time, put under the arrest, as you Americans say."

Jane's interest was piqued. "She'd been arrested? For what?"

Madame Hulot shook her head. "I cannot remember. Drugs, perhaps? Isn't that what makes all young people go to the jail these days?"

"Oh my!" Hillary said, glancing at Jane. "Another connection to—"

"Ah, I know what you are thinking," Madame Hulot interrupted. "That is what poor Guillaume was arrested for. Drugs." She shook her head and looked as if she might cry. "But I cannot believe it. Not Guillaume Daudet. He is the son of my husband's cousin. A good boy. His family has made wine in Lenoir for centuries. Not drugs. Why would he want to do that when he can make the wine? It is impossible! He was making enough of the money. He has young children. A beautiful wife. He would not do this. Not Guillaume. *Impossible!*" Again, she gave the word the French pronunciation. Still shaking her head, she mounted her bike again. "I do not understand all that has happened. It has never been this way in Lenoir before," she said, pedaling away. "We are a peaceful village." She turned back to call over her shoulder. "We will resume the class the day after tomorrow. May God protect you!"

"Didn't I tell you?" Hillary said as she and Jane walked toward the door. "Didn't I say Eugenie was mixed up in it some way?"

"You did say that, Hill, but then you also built quite a case for Lola killing Henry out of jealousy."

"Oh well," Hillary said, brushing it off with one of her waves, "so I was wrong about Lola and right about Daudet and Eugenie. But I still say there was something fishy going on between Henry and that girl."

"You have no proof of that, Hillary. You don't even have evidence. You're just guessing."

"What do you call lying together in that chapel if it's not evidence?" Hillary sounded indignant.

"That's not evidence." Jane was insistent. "There could be numerous reasons why those two were there. I told you, they could have been placed there by whoever killed them. They could have been—"

"Jane, Jane, Jane, sometimes all of your law school logic just gets in the way of common sense. After all, you only had a semester or two of law school. You just don't want to admit that I outsmarted you on this one."

Jane didn't have time to argue. By now they had reached

the front door, and Beau, who had gone into the house through the back, met them there, along with Buddy and Shakura and Sarah.

"You have another telegram," Beau said, handing Hillary a yellow envelope.

"It came while y'all was gone, but I never opened it." Buddy's curiosity kept him hovering over them, which confirmed to Jane that he had been tempted to open it.

"I never knew what a telegram was before," Sarah said.

"Me neither," Shakura said. "But I've heard of them. From watching those old movies my mom watches."

"Why do people send telegrams anyway, Mom?" Sarah asked. "Can't they just E-mail?"

"Not without a telephone," Shakura reminded her.

"It's from Billy!" Hillary waved the telegram excitedly. "He's flying into Monte Carlo tomorrow, and he wants us to meet him there."

Jane felt a mix of emotions roiling inside her. "That's wonderful, but since the girls didn't get their trip to Les Baux today, I was hoping we could do that tomorrow."

Hillary had a troubled look on her face. "I can't just leave Billy waiting at the airport."

"I know," Jane said, "but to disappoint the girls two days in a row . . . Maybe you could just drop us off at the ruins on the way to Monte Carlo, then pick us up after—"

"It's a long drive to Monte Carlo," Beau said. "You'd have more time at the ruins than you'd know what to do with."

"Then you'll just have to rent another car, Hill," Jane said.

Hillary nodded. "Well, of course. Why didn't I think of that? I'll rent the car and leave the van for the rest of you."

Jane's suggestion seemed a perfect solution until the next morning when Hillary showed up in Jane's room before breakfast wearing her feathery high-heeled bedroom slippers and her brocade robe.

Jane, wearing the oversized T-shirt she used for a nightgown, her eyes half-closed, and her voice hoarse from sleep, let Hillary in.

"What is it, Hillary? Is something wrong? Don't tell me there was someone in your room again."

"Oh no, nothing like that." Hillary stood in the middle of the room, toying with the sleeve of her robe.

"Then what is it?" Jane tried to will away the morning taste in her mouth.

"It's . . . well, it's just that I can't go to Monte Carlo alone. I mean this is a foreign country. I can't read the road signs. What if I get lost?"

Jane gave her a suspicious look. "What are you saying, Hillary?"

"You have to go with me, Jane. I can't do it alone."

"But—"

"I'm just asking you to help me out. After all, it's what I pay you for, and anyway, I should think that as a friend you would—"

"OK, Hillary."

"Well, that you would want to help me out, because—"

"I said OK, Hill."

"What? You mean you'll—"

"I'll go with you. I'll ask Beau to take the girls."

"Oh, Jane, you don't know how much I appreciate this."

"Yeah, well, you're right, it *is* my job and you *are* my friend."

"You won't regret this, Jane." Hillary gave her a happy smile as she started for the door. "I'll see that you get a bonus and plenty of time later to spend with the girls."

"I don't need a bonus to do a friend a favor," Jane called to her as the door closed. "And I already regret it," she said to the door. The truth was, she really didn't want Hillary driving all the way to Monte Carlo alone. She had been thinking of asking Beau to go along with Hillary, but since Hillary had asked her, she couldn't refuse. It was her job, as Hillary had said, and more importantly, she was her friend.

• • •

The next afternoon, Sarah and Shakura were excited about seeing the ruins, and in particular the reproductions of ancient battering rams and catapults on the fields outside the castle ruins. Buddy was torn between going with Jane to see after her and going with Sarah. He just couldn't make up his mind at first, just which way "ol' Jim Ed" would want him to go.

In the end, he chose to go with Sarah. "I'm sorry, but I better go with her," he said to Jane, sounding apologetic. "I ain't happy about you being alone in some foreign place, but then, I ain't never met a cop I could trust, and I sure ain't going to trust him to watch out for Jim Ed's little girl."

"I'll be fine," Jane assured him. "Go with Sarah and have a good time."

"This ain't about having a good time, Miz Ferguson. I'm doin' it for—"

"I know, Buddy, I know. You're doing it for Jim Ed."

"Well, somebody's got to look after you and Sarah."

"And you're the man, Buddy, you're the man." Jane's tone carried a note of resignation.

Buddy's brow was creased with a troubled frown, as if he still wasn't sure he'd made the right decision. "You just be careful, you hear?" He, like Beau, pronounced the word, *heah*.

"I'll be careful, Buddy. I promise."

Hillary had arranged to rent a small Citroën for the drive to Monte Carlo so Beau, Buddy, and the girls could take the van on their outing. Beau was loading the van with picnic supplies while Hillary was still inside getting dressed.

She emerged at last wearing off-white linen slacks with a matching jacket and a deep-coral silk shell. She'd applied nail polish to match the shell, and her thick, dark auburn hair was combed into a smooth, chic style.

Jane was dressed in jeans and sandals and a white cotton blouse, tied at the midriff to reveal just a little skin. She was dressed for comfort and had given in long ago to the fact that she would always be in Hillary's shadow where fashion was concerned.

"Oh, I can hardly wait to see Billy," Hillary said as she walked toward the car. "His plane arrives at six, and Beau says it's about a three-hour drive, so after we meet him at the airport, we'll have time for dinner at one of those posh restaurants on the Riviera." She scrutinized Jane. "Jane, dear, you must grab something else to take along to change into. There's bound to be a dress code at some of the restaurants, and I'm sure you want to measure up."

"Hillary, nothing I own will measure up to the Monte Carlo jet set crowd," Jane protested, but she went back to her room and retrieved a hunter green linen miniskirt, along with a pair of gold sandals she'd bought on sale at Penney's. She tossed them in the backseat of the tiny car and was about to slide into the driver's seat when Hillary stopped her.

"Jane, dear, I'm afraid I'll have to drive."

"But Hillary—"

"I'm the only designated driver on the rental agreement. You have to pay an extra fee for the second driver, and I couldn't imagine that you'd want to drive anyway."

"Oh sure," Jane mumbled as she walked around to the passenger side of the car. "I enjoy putting my life on the line."

"What was that, Jane?"

"I, uh, said we've got to get started if we want to get there on time."

Jane gave Sarah a quick kiss just before she scrambled to her seat next to Shakura in the van, then got into the car with Hillary. They sped away, bumping over a small bush that had been planted in an unfortunate spot along the side of the driveway and sprayed gravel as they lurched onto the pavement. They made two complete circles on the roundabout at heart-stopping speed before Hillary at last launched them on the road to Arles.

Jane kept her eyes closed most of the way, preferring not to see the trucks loaded with farm produce coming at them head-on when Hillary was in the passing lane or the intersections whose stop signs Hillary all too often ignored.

"I'm so anxious for you to meet Billy. And it worked out just perfectly that one of his clients happens to be in Monte Carlo. We can go shopping while he meets with the client, then we'll have our little outing and drive back together. Open your eyes, Jane. That truck missed us by six inches. Billy says he can't wait to meet you. And he knows the most wonderful places in Monte Carlo."

"I'm eager to meet him, as well," Jane said, still not opening her eyes.

"Oh look, Jane, there's lavender growing along the side of the road."

"Uh-huh."

"You didn't look."

"Yes, I did." Jane gave a quick glance out the window. She saw no lavender, but her eye did catch the reflection of a small black car in the side mirror. It was following alarmingly close.

"What's that car doing so close behind us, Hillary?"

"What car?" As Hillary spoke, she touched the brakes, slowing the Citroën. The car behind them had no choice but to brake. They heard its brakes squeal as it tried to avoid hitting them. It swerved wildly toward the edge of the road, and then finally off the road in a cloud of dust and gravel. "Why, I have no idea," Hillary said, "but it's certainly someone who doesn't know the first thing about driving." She sped away, leaving the black car behind, spinning its wheels, trying to get out of the ditch.

Once they were on the divided highway headed toward Monte Carlo, Jane relaxed a little. At least there were no stop signs to run or oncoming traffic.

Jane saw Hillary glance at her as she changed lanes without signaling. "Is something wrong, Jane?"

Jane shook her head. "No, I was just thinking about what

Madame Hulot said. She seemed pretty convinced that Daudet couldn't be a murderer or mixed up in drugs."

Hillery took one hand off the wheel long enough to inspect her manicure. "Isn't that always the way? The ones you least expect . . ."

"I still say something just doesn't seem to fit," Jane said. "I just don't see how Daudet could have had a meth lab in his winery. We toured every square inch of the place. And if Paul Hayes and Henry and Eugenie saw it, why didn't we?"

"Well, my Lord, Jane, he could have had it hidden behind some of that machinery or something."

"Maybe, but . . ."

Hillary glanced at her again. "But what?"

"It just doesn't feel right."

"Are you saying we need to investigate?" There was a hint of excitement in Hillary's voice.

Jane waited just a little too long to reply.

"Where do you think we should start? I mean, if Daudet didn't do it, then who? Oh, I know I mentioned Lola, but I was wrong about that, of course. She wouldn't kill her own husband, would she? So, who?"

"I don't know, but I wasn't implying that we—"

"Oh my Lord!" Hillary said, interrupting her. Hillary's eyes were fixed on the rearview mirror.

"What?"

"That car. Isn't it kind of strange that it's still following us?"

Jane turned around to see the car behind them. The slope of the windshield made it impossible to see who was inside, but the car, a Renault, looked familiar to Jane. Then suddenly, the car rammed them from behind, sending both Jane and Hillary lurching forward.

Hillary screamed and accelerated, and Jane felt her stomach do a flip-flop.

The car easily matched Hillary's speed. It caught up with her, then swerved around her and slowed, so that the two cars were traveling side by side. Then the window on the passenger side of the Renault lowered slightly, and Jane watched as the unmistakable dark steel barrel of a gun emerged.

There was a loud explosion, a momentary spray of red fire, and Hillary's scream.

10

Everything seemed to happen at once. The Citroën lurched forward as Hillary screamed and hit the accelerator, swerving twice to maneuver around two cars, one on the left, and one on the right. At the same time, there was a piercing screech above Jane's and Hillary's heads as a bullet grazed the top of the car.

"Oh dear!" Hillary said, leaning forward, hunched over the steering wheel.

"Shit!" Jane said, sliding down low in the seat.

"Who *was* that?" Hillary's voice was high-pitched with fear, her bloodless face tense. She went around another car, cutting in so quickly, she narrowly missed hitting it. At the angry blast of the driver's horn, she accelerated again.

Jane dared to inch upward and glance out the rear window. The dark Renault was still there, though a few cars behind then now.

"You're losing them! Keep going, Hill!"

Hillary's high-heeled pump came down hard on the accelerator, and her tires screeched as she whipped around yet another car, forcing a small truck in the left lane to veer off the road onto the divider. It did them little good; there were cars blocking all three lanes in front of her. That didn't stop her, though. She skittered around the car in the left lane, forcing both left tires of the Citroën up on the divider, tilting the car. She dropped off the median with a hard thump and cut diagonally across the autoroute, headed for the far right lane. Again horns blared, and Jane could hear one or two muffled angry shouts.

And then the roiling sea of sound was grudgingly calmed by the high-pitched wavering whine of authority, a siren.

Jane turned around again to look out the back window. "Geez, Hill, it's the cops. They're after us."

Hillary kept her eyes straight ahead, not bothering to check the rearview mirror. "Nonsense. Why would they be coming after us? If they're after anyone, it's the people who shot at us." She turned the steering wheel suddenly, throwing Jane against the door as she careened down an exit ramp.

Jane glanced to the rear again. The police apparently had not heard the gunshots and had not seen the incident. What caught their attention was Hillary's crazy maneuvering; the police car was still pursuing them. Jane braced herself for whatever Hillary was going to plow into at the high rate of speed she was traveling. "Christ, Hillary, where are you going?"

Hillary sped ahead, a determined look on her face. "I'm trying to lose those crazy people with the guns while the police are after them." The ramp took them, like a storm drain, into another torrent of traffic. Hillary made a quick left, and Jane made another quick glance behind them.

"It's the cops who are after us, Hill."

"They can't be." Hillary made another turn, merging into a stream of traffic trickling down a narrow street. Jane could still hear the *wah, wah, wah* of the siren somewhere in the distance.

Hillary exited to another street and rolled down a hill and through a valley of crumbling storefronts toward a tunnel. By the time they entered the tunnel, the sound of the siren had been absorbed by the metallic clank of the city.

"I think the policeman must have got them," Hillary said.

"I tell you, that cop was after us." Jane's head was pounding, out of rhythm with the pounding of her heart.

"Oh well," Hillary said with a little shrug. She slowed a bit and looked around her at the street. "Where are we?"

"How the hell should I know?"

"Jane, I was depending on you. I mean, if I'm doing the driving, I shouldn't be expected to know where I'm going."

Jane looked at Hillary, speechless. Sometimes it was best not to comment on Hillary's logic. Instead, she glanced out the window at the row of crumbling buildings with laundry hanging outside windows, old cars, and children with a look in their eyes expressing a hunger more profound than a need for food.

In a short time, the blight gave way to storefronts with a modestly prosperous look and then apartment buildings and more storefronts with the look of affluence. Still on a back road, they drove a short distance through the country-side until they came to another town shimmering in ancient grandeur. They wound through the town and into the country again and finally into yet another town. The sun was sinking low on the horizon when at last the sea stretched in front of them, winking at itself in the late-afternoon light and lapping at the white shore like a cat licking the toes of its master.

"Oh my God!" Jane's voice was barely above a whisper. "It's beautiful!"

Hillary stopped the car at the side of the road. "That color! That incredible blue! If I could just get that in a drapery fabric!"

"And look! Over there!" Jane pointed to something in front of them. "Isn't that the casino?"

"We're in Monte Carlo!"

Jane glanced around. "And we seem to have lost the bad guys as well as the police."

"Thank God." Hillary still looked shaken. "Who were those guys, anyway?"

"I don't know, but this is getting too scary. I think we should go to the police right now and tell them what happened."

Hillary looked at her watch. "But we can't, lamb. We have to pick up Billy in fifteen minutes. Then we can go to the police. It will be better to have Billy with us, anyway. He always knows how to handle things."

"Great, we'll let Billy handle it. But which way is the airport?"

Hillary gave her a troubled look. "I told you, I was depending on you."

The throb in Jane's head intensified. "Hillary, how can I make you understand? I can't find my way around someplace I've never been before."

"We can't be lost, Jane. We don't have time. Billy's plane arrives in fifteen minutes."

"Then we'll just have to ask somebody."

"Who?"

Jane pointed to the beach. "How about one of those sunbathers down there? At least one of them has to speak English."

Hillary started the car and pulled onto the street, headed for the beach. "OK, but we've got to find someone fast. Billy doesn't like to be kept waiting."

It took several minutes to find a parking space, but Hillary finally managed to squeeze the Citroën next to a gold Porsche. There was barely room to open one door, and Jane had to scoot across the seat to the driver's side to get out. Once on the street, she saw that there was less than half an inch clearance for the Porsche. Hillary hadn't bothered to look. She was already crossing the street, headed for the beach.

"Can you believe this, Jane? We are actually walking along the Riviera! This is where the jet set plays. Why, if we look closely, I'll bet we can even find a movie star to

ask for directions to the airport. Maybe Nicole Kidman or
Tom Cruise, or maybe even—oh my God! Jane!" Hillary
grabbed Jane's arm. "Those people are . . . Oh Lord, lamb!"

"This is the Riviera, Hillary. The women go topless."

"Well, yes, of course I knew that. It's just that I had no
idea they would look so . . . well, *naked!*"

Jane glanced around at the crowd, which seemed to be
one multilimbed and multibreasted copper-colored beast
shifting on its haunches. "I don't see Tom or Nicole around
anywhere, so who shall we ask?"

Hillary took a deep breath and leaned toward a deeply
bronzed woman lying on a beach towel whose only clothing
was a narrow strip of gold lamé several inches below her
belly button. "Excuse me, ma'am, could y'all tell me where
the airport is?"

The woman answered by lifting her Gucci sunglasses just
long enough to give Hillary a disdainful look before she
lay down again and tilted her face to the dying sun.

"Well, where did you learn your manners? Not in Prosper, Alabama, that's for sure." Hillary turned away in a
huff.

Jane glanced over her shoulder, looking for another
likely candidate. What she saw made fear sprout and twitch
in her veins. "Hillary . . ." Hillary, Jane saw when she
turned around again, was walking toward a glistening male
body on a beach chair.

"I don't know what she has to be so stuck up about,
anyway." Hillary threw the words over her shoulder at Jane.
Jane grabbed Hillary's arm and tried to pull her away. "I
mean, I was president of the garden club for two consec-
utive terms and a past president of Junior League and a
Kappa besides. What are you doing, Jane?"

"Hillary, we've got to get out of here!"

"We don't know the way to the airport yet. I'm sure there
must be someone here who—"

"They're here, Hillary. On the beach!"

"Who?"

"Those guys who followed us."

"How do you know? We didn't even see their faces."

"There's their car. Double-parked in front of ours." Jane was pulling Hillary along, headed away from the cars. "And don't look now, but there are two guys in dark suits behind us. It has to be them. They're the only ones out here besides us who're dressed."

In spite of Jane's warning, Hillary glanced over her shoulder. "Oh my Lord, they're coming toward us!" Hillary quickly removed her high heels and ran in stocking feet across the sandy beach to a stairway that led up to the street. Jane, also running, passed her and reached the stairs first.

By the time they reached the top of the stairs, the two men were mounting the bottom steps. Hillary barely had time to put her shoes on before Jane pulled her into a crush of pedestrians and then into the street where they found themselves in a discordant mix of screaming tires and angry horns until they were finally on the other side.

Jane could see the men across the street coming toward them. "Come on!" she said. They kept moving, and Jane glanced back only once. It was enough to see that the men, too, had crossed the street. "They're behind us again." She was out of breath, and the air around them was hot and gummy.

"What are we going to do?" Hillary's eyes were round with fear.

"Keep moving." Jane took Hillary's hand and ran until they reached the edge of a park, then she pulled Hillary into a maze of trees.

Hillary pulled back, let go of Jane's hand, and looked around. "This has got to be a dangerous place, Jane. We could get mugged. We've got to get out of here."

"It's no more dangerous than out there on the streets, Hill."

Hillary spotted a park bench, partly obscured by trees.

She walked to it and sat down wearily. "I just wish I knew who those men are."

Jane sat down beside her. The heat was making her feel tired, too. "It has to have something to do with those three murders. Someone must think we know something, and they want to get rid of us."

Hillary looked at her. "Then maybe I should just tell them we don't know anything and to leave us alone."

"Oh yeah, sure, you do that."

"Are you being cynical again?"

"They shot at us, Hill. That tells me they're not in any mood to listen."

Hillary gave Jane a worried look, then reached in her handbag for a tissue and mopped her face. "You've got to get us out of this, Jane. This heat will clog my pores."

Jane had gotten up to peer around the trees for any sight of the men. "If I'd known your pores were going to clog, I'd have gotten us out of this long ago." She threw the words at Hillary over her shoulder.

"That's right, Jane. Go ahead and make fun of me while my life is in danger and my poor husband is waiting at the airport, wondering where I am." Hillary's voice trembled.

Jane came back to the bench and sat down heavily beside Hillary. "Don't be so self-centered, Hillary. My life is in danger, too, and I'm scared shitless."

"Don't say that, Jane. We can't afford for both of us to be frightened, and must you use such language?"

Jane glanced at Hillary and saw just how scared she was. Her hands were trembling, and she looked as if she was about to cry. Both of them were silent for a long time. Finally, Hillary spoke.

"What are you thinking, Jane?"

"I'm thinking," Jane said, "that there is more to this than a couple of people stumbling on a small-time meth lab, and I still don't think Daudet killed those people. I think he's just a scapegoat."

"Then who did it? And why?"

"If we could just talk to those guys who are following us, maybe we could find out."

Hillary gasped. "You're not serious are you, lamb? You just said yourself, they're dangerous."

Jane sighed. "Of course not."

There was another long silence until Hillary spoke again. "Sitting on a park bench scared to death is not the way I thought I'd spend my vacation."

"I hope Sarah and Shakura are all right. They'll be worried when I don't show up on time."

"I was going to practice preparing the canapés Madame Hulot taught us to do last time. Billy loves canapés."

Jane gave up. Hillary was better at non sequiturs than she was.

In a little while, Hillary said, "It's getting dark and scary, Jane."

Jane looked around her. Hillary was right, it was getting dark, and Jane was becoming more and more uneasy. She stood up once again and searched beyond the trees. There was no one in sight. "Let's try to make it back to the car," she said.

Hillary stood and reached for her hand. Together, they walked, stumbling occasionally in the growing darkness, back to the sidewalk that encircled the park.

As soon as they reached the sidewalk, Hillary sucked in her breath. "Oh my Lord! It's them."

Jane glanced in the direction Hillary was pointing and saw the two men, less than a half block away, coming toward them.

Jane grabbed Hillary's hand and pulled her. "Come on! Run!"

"Where?"

"There!" Jane pointed in front of her. The casino spread itself in ornate Moorish grandeur before them.

Hillary pulled back on Jane's hand. "I can't."

"You have to, Hillary. There'll be crowds in there. They can't shoot us in a crowd. I hope."

"But . . ."

Jane yanked at Hillary again, forcing her to trot along beside her. "If it's some kind of religious thing, don't worry about it. We're not going in there to gamble."

"I'm not religious, Jane, I'm Episcopalian."

"Then what!" Jane screeched when she felt Hillary holding back again.

"I'm not dressed for that place."

Jane gave her a hard jerk. "Oh for Christ's sake!"

"I've seen this place on TV and in all those James Bond movies. I've seen the way people dress in there. A person can't be seen in there in something that costs less than a few thousand dollars."

In spite of Hillary's protest, Jane was still pulling her along, up the stairs and into the entrance hall of the gilded gambling palace.

A few tourists milled around on the plush scarlet carpet of the front lobby, and Jane could hear the clank and rattle of the slot machines in the small room to the right where street tourists dropped coins into the machines just for the thrill of saying they'd gambled in the Monte Carlo casino. In front of them was the entrance to the traditional gaming rooms, guarded by a doorman in a dark suit.

Jane was unsure what to do, but when she saw their pursuers through one of the grand windows, Jane turned quickly to Hillary and grabbed her hand again. "Come on, we've got to hide somewhere."

"Where?" Hillary was breathless, and Jane could feel her hand trembling.

"In there." She pointed to the gaming rooms.

"But that man standing there . . ." Hillary seemed reluctant. "I think you have to pay or something. We at least have to be dressed."

Ahead of them, an American couple dressed in shorts and straw hats were trying to get in.

"I am very sorry," the doorman said in textbook English. "But you must be dressed to enter the casino."

"Hell, we are dressed, and our money's good as any-body's," the man said.

"Oh my Lord! There's a woman in there having a baby. On the floor!" It was Hillary screaming and pointing toward the slot room for street tourists. The doorman grew wide-eyed as Hillary moved toward him, took his arm and pulled him away from his post. "You've got to help her!"

"I will call security, madame," the doorman said.

"Now!" Hillary cried. "You've got to help her now!"

The doorman looked confused for a moment, gave a quick command to the man behind a counter, then hurried away to the slot room. The counter man picked up a tele-phone, and Hillary pulled Jane toward the door to the main gaming room.

Behind them, the casually dressed American couple looked on, wide-eyed.

The opulence of crystal chandeliers, golden with light, ornately carved ceilings, walls hung with exquisite paint-ings, and plush velvet drapes, along with the murmuring, click-clacking sound of the room, left Jane gaping for a moment, but she quickly moved with Hillary into the depths of the palace. "That was quick thinking, Hill. You were great!"

They maneuvered their way around a maze of men and women seated at gaming tables, all looking suntanned, trim, and fashionably bored as they placed their bets, threw the dice, and gave up their money. The dress was elegant and expensive and, for the women at least, scant. Several of them gave Jane what seemed to her to be a look of disap-proval when they noticed her jeans and sturdy sandals.

"Did they follow us in?" Hillary's voice was shaking.

"I don't know, but I don't think—Oh my God, there they are!" Jane ducked behind an ornate pillar, pulling Hillary with her.

"Maybe we should just go ask them what they want." Hillary was whispering and sticking close to Jane.

"Are you crazy? They tried to kill us!"

"I've been thinking, Jane. You see, there's no reason to kill us. It has to be a case of mistaken identity. I'm sure if we just confront them, they'll realize it's someone else they want to kill."

"It's us they want, Hillary. They got a good look at both of us and tried to shoot us." She pulled Hillary toward a series of doors on the wall nearest them. Opening the door, she quickly stepped inside, still holding Hillary's hand.

They had entered another ornate room full of long tables. People sat around them while others stood by, watching. Each table was also graced by the presence of three men in tuxedos. Jane had watched enough James Bond movies herself to know they had entered the gilded and exclusive pit of chemin de fer players. She moved with Hillary, deep into the room, trying to blend in with the crowd, pretending to be interested in watching the players and all the while keeping her eyes on the door.

The crowd at the tables seemed to be constantly shifting, making Jane and Hillary move from side to side. Jane also found that the two of them were moving closer and closer to the table until, at last, Hillary was standing next to the table with Jane directly behind her.

"Have you seen them yet?" Hillary whispered over her shoulder to Jane.

"Not yet, but I'm not sure we're out of danger. They could still find their way in here."

"What are we going to do?" Hillary sounded near tears.

"Just try to blend in." Jane touched Hillary's shoulder. "I'm going to try to make my way to that table over there where I'll have a better view. I want to make sure they're not in here."

"You've got to get us out of here, Jane. We're already late. Billy will be wondering where we are."

"Believe me, Hill, nobody wants out of here any more than I do." Jane leaned closer to Hillary. "Hang in there. I'll be right back."

She edged her way through the crowd standing behind

her and surveyed the room before she dared to make her
way to a table nearer the door. She had just moved next to
a tall, breathtakingly thin woman, her skin hardened from
the sun. She wore tight-fitting pants and a short-cropped,
sleeveless, and loose-fitting jeweled top, the kind of outfit
Jane had only seen on cable television when CNN showed
the Paris fashions.

Jane coughed when the woman's cigarette smoke accosted her, but the woman ignored her and turned her sur-
gically lifted and stretched face and her crew-cut spiked
hair away to watch the banker draw a card from the shoe.
The noise in the room had grown louder, and there was a
particularly loud murmur of excitement emanating period-
ically from the table where she left Hillary.

Jane welcomed the increased noise and the heightening
sense of excitement and tension in the room. She hoped
that meant she would be less likely to be noticed. She surveyed the room, searching for the two faceless men in dark
coats who had followed her and Hillary.

She was beginning to feel more relaxed until the door
opened and two men entered—the same two men she'd
seen in the main room of the casino earlier and, she was
sure, the same men who had shot at her and Hillary. They
wore dark suits, one a deep brown and the other a dark
shade of green. Both were of medium build, and there was
something distinctly odd about their faces, both shaded by
hats with the brim turned down. On closer look, Jane saw
that the men were wearing tight-fitting rubber masks, the
kind children wear on Halloween.

Jane felt an unpleasant but all-too-familiar knot in her
stomach as the men surveyed the room. She tried to dis-
appear behind a tall man in an expensive suit. She had to
warn Hillary. She edged away from the table, trying to fall
in step with a couple ambling across the room, praying that
the men wouldn't spot her.

Finally, she made her way to the table where she'd left
Hillary. The crowd around the table had grown, and so had

the level of excitement. Someone was on a winning streak. She and Hillary would have to move away quickly, because the excited atmosphere around this particular table was sure to draw the attention of the two mysterious men.

Jane searched for Hillary in the crowd and finally saw her auburn hair. She was still on the front lines next to the table. Jane elbowed her way through the crush of people until she was directly behind her.

"Hillary, come on, we've got to try to get out of here." Jane spoke in an urgent whisper.

Hillary didn't answer.

"Hillary!"

Still no answer. It was then that Jane saw Hillary's hand move to the shoe to remove a card, at a command in French from one of the men in a tuxedo. Hillary placed the card facedown in front of the man. At another command, she pulled another card from the shoe and tucked it under the shoe.

"Hillary, what are you doing? Come on, we've got to get out of here."

"Not now, Jane, I'm busy!" Hillary and the tuxedo man were repeating the same ritualistic sequence with the commands and the cards.

"Are you crazy?"

"I'm just blending in."

"Christ, Hillary, you're playing the most dangerous game in Europe." Jane glanced over her shoulder again, looking for the men. "In more ways than one."

There was another ritualistic sequence in which someone else at the table was allowed to look at the tuxedo man's hand. The man in the tuxedo said, *"Sept,"* then signaled something to Hillary. She removed the cards from under the shoe, tossed them to the man in the tuxedo, who announced, *"Neuf!"* and the crowd's twitter grew to an excited crescendo. An enormous stack of chips appeared in front of Hillary.

Jane grabbed Hillary's arm. "That's it! We're out of here."

Hillary seemed to pull back. "But Jane, it isn't polite to leave when you're winning." She was doing her best to scoop up her chips, but Jane kept pulling at her until she had her away from the table. Chips were falling out of Hillary's overfilled purse.

"They're here! We've got to find some way to get out of this room!" Jane led Hillary toward the door, but it was too late. In the next moment, two menacing hulks were standing directly in front of them, blocking the door.

"I beg your pardon, but you are standing in my way!" Hillary's voice dripped its Southern accent. "And both of you have been acting just real tacky.

One of the men reached out to grab Hillary, and she raised her hand to push his away. In the same instant, a uniformed policeman appeared, and a metal ring closed around Hillary's wrist with a sickening click. In the next moment, Jane felt someone pull both her arms behind her, and her wrists were handcuffed as well. The men in dark coats appeared momentarily puzzled and then hurried away.

"Je vous arrête," a voice said in French, and then in English, "You are under arrest."

11

"Remove these awful things from my wrists!" Hillary used her Scarlett O'Hara voice.

"You are under arrest, Madame." The policeman, a short, heavy man, had to look up to meet Hillary's eyes.

"Of course I'm not under arrest. I'm Hillary Scarborough from Prosper, Alabama. I have my own television show, and I'm the past president of the Prosper Junior League, a Kappa, and my grandmother was a Spencer. An *Atlanta* Spencer, I'll have you know!"

"And I am Henri Bonnette, a member of the police force of Monte Carlo in the Principality of Monaco, and you are still under arrest!" The short little man was bouncing on the balls of his feet as he spoke to Hillary.

"But I can't be. You have the wrong—"

The little policeman took Hillary's arm and pulled her toward the door while another policeman ushered Jane along behind them.

"Even in Monte Carlo we have a right to know what the charges are, don't we?" Jane was speaking to the policeman who seemed to be responsible for her. He was an older man with thinning gray hair and a craggy face. He looked straight ahead, ignoring her, as he spoke in French to the shorter man.

"Marcel does not speak English," the short man said. "You are charged with . . . um, in English it is called attempting robbery."

"Robbery!" Jane and Hillary said together.

"We have been watching you. The French police suspect you are on zee run after robbing a bank in Nice when they saw you on the autoroute driving beyond the speed limit. They radio us. Then when you came here, we watch you hide in the park. And then! We think you must be planning to rob the casino and we will catch you, with the red hands."

"You mean red-handed," Hillary said.

The policeman streched his neck to look her in the eyes. "Ah yes, red-handed. Then when you sneak in, we know we have you."

Jane tried to protest, but the little policeman cut her off. "No more talk. You are very clever, of course, but you will not fool us again. You are going to the jail."

"Jail! You wouldn't dare!" Hillary had a desperate look in her eyes. "Jane, do something!"

"Believe me, Hillary, if I knew what to do—"

"No more talk," the little policeman barked again. He led them out of the elaborate casino building, their hands shackled in the irons of justice behind their backs. A crowd of onlookers gawked at them, and someone shouted something in French. Jane couldn't understand the words, but judging from the tone of voice, she would like to have replied with the appropriate gesture.

"Listen, sir . . ." Hillary's voice was warm Southern molasses as she spoke to the policeman again, trying another tactic. "I just think you should know that we were trying to contact y'all all along because of what happened on the autoroute, and the only reason we're in this place is because we were trying to get away from—"

"I said no more talk!" the short little bulldog man barked as he shoved Hillary into the car, none too gently.

Jane saw Hillary's eyes turn to her, silent and pleading as they sat side by side in the back of the police car. It was a decidedly uncomfortable position Jane found herself in, having to lean forward slightly because of her hands locked behind her back. Hillary looked equally uncomfortable.

The two policemen got into the front seat of the police car, the short one in the driver's seat.

Hillary leaned forward to speak to him. "How are we going to be able to put our seat belts on with our hands behind our backs like this? Passenger safety has always been one of my priorities when I'm driving, and I'm sure you feel the same about—"

The policeman reached one of his short, thick arms behind him and raised the bulletproof shield separating the front seat from the back before Hillary could finish her sentence.

Hillary settled into the seat with a look of frustration on her face. "I declare, I have never seen anything like this. Doesn't anybody in this town have any manners?"

"I wouldn't be worrying about whether or not these people have been to charm school, Hillary," Jane said. "We've got other things to worry about. We are in deep doo-doo."

"Well we wouldn't be, if they would just let me explain." Hillary had her wide-eyed, pale-faced look again, the look that always made Jane worry. "Jane!" Hillary's troubled frown deepened. "Don't just sit there. You're supposed to say something comforting."

"Like what?" Jane, in truth, was doing her best to think of something comforting.

"I don't know. Something legal. Something like, we'll be all right, Hillary, because it's illegal for the Monacoan police to arrest people from Alabama. I mean, isn't there some kind of international treaty or something?"

"If there's a treaty between Monaco and Alabama, it escaped my notice."

"Well, after all, you didn't finish law school. There's bound to be something."

"Hillary—"

"What are we going to do, Jane? Please tell me what we're going to do. Billy will be frantic."

And so will Sarah, Jane thought, but she didn't say it aloud.

"What are we going to do?" Hillary said again, her voice filled with desperation as she choked back tears.

"I'm sure everything will be all right," Jane lied.

"We'll tell them you're a lawyer. We'll tell them about Jim Ed being a lawyer," Hillary said, her eyes brightening a little now that she was beginning to formulate a plan.

A sardonic laugh escaped from Jane. "What good is it going to do to tell them about Jim Ed when your Atlanta bloodlines didn't even faze them?"

"That's a good point," Hillary mused, serious in spite of Jane's sarcasm. "You can bet that if Princess Grace was still alive, they wouldn't be able to get by with this. I'm sure *she* knew about bloodlines."

"Oh yeah, and she was probably a Kappa, too, and that would have been our ticket out for sure."

Hillary raised an eyebrow. "Really? I always thought she looked more like the Tri-Delt type."

Jane rolled her eyes and bit her tongue to keep from saying something even more sarcastic. No point in adding to Hillary's misery.

By now they had reached the police station, an ancient building with a dark facade on a street full of more old buildings.

"What are they going to do to us, Jane?" Hillary appeared anxious again, now that the policemen were getting out of the car and preparing to pull the two of them out of the backseat. "I mean, we're entitled to have a lawyer, aren't we? Don't we get our rights read to us and a phone call?"

"I told you, we're not in Kansas anymore, Hillary. The

Constitution doesn't apply, and they never heard of the Miranda Law. For all I know, they can throw us in a dungeon for a decade or two."

"Oh my Lord, Jane, a person has to get their nails done more often than that." Hillary sounded as if she was about to cry as the back doors opened and the policemen reached in to grab them.

"Good point, Hill," Jane said over her shoulder as she was pulled out of the car. "I think you should mention that at the trial. If there is a trial."

"I am trying to be patient with you, Jane," Hillary said. The short-legged policeman who held her arm was forced to scurry along as Hillary tried to catch up with the officer dragging Jane along. "I know you get worse when you're upset, but you have got to get ahold of yourself and get us out of this mess. At least find some way to get in touch with Billy. He'll know what to do."

"You will stop talking!" the little bulldog barked again.

Hillary turned to him in all of her fury, and in spite of the fact that her hands were shackled behind her, managed to look both regal and indignant. "You hush up now, I have got things to talk about with Jane, and you are beginning to get on my nerves!"

The startled policeman stared at Hillary without saying a word. Hillary turned with an impatient huff back to Jane.

"Just talk to them, Jane," she whispered. "Say something legal. Tell them they don't have any right to hold American citizens. Remind them that we were allies during the war. We were, weren't we? Oh well, it doesn't matter, tell them anyway. Tell them we want to call the airport. We'll ask for Billy. We'll have him paged. He'll get us out of this."

"I'll do the best I can." Jane's whisper was edged with both irritation and worry. "Just let me do the talking."

"Ordinarily, I would, Jane, but you just seem so reluctant now. I don't know what's wrong with you."

"I told you, the rules are different here. I'm just going

to have to figure this out. All I know for sure is you piss them off, so let me handle it, OK?"

"Just don't mess it up," Hillary whispered as they stepped into the cavernous, dank building, "and try to use more elegant language."

In spite of the fact that the room, much like police stations in the U.S., was filled with bureaucrats behind desks, Jane couldn't quite get rid of the sensation that she had walked into a torture chamber from the Middle Ages.

"I'll take care of this, Hillary, don't worry." Jane spoke with exaggerated confidence. "They'll take us to a booking officer, who'll want to ask us some questions. You know, name, citizenship, maybe Social Security number. The officer will have to speak English, of course, so I'll just explain what happened, and—"

"Tell them about the car on the autoroute, and explain that we were only trying—"

"I said I'll take care of it, Hillary. Just don't worry."

Ten minutes later, Jane and Hillary were inside a narrow cell with two bunk beds, a toilet, and a sink. They were wearing orange jumpsuits. There had been no booking officer. There had been no chance to explain anything.

For the next several hours, Hillary alternated between a despair marked by deep sighs and a pale, expressionless face. She paced the floor wondering aloud where Billy was and how anyone would ever find out where they were and lamenting that she didn't look good in orange.

"They behead people here. You think I don't know that?" she said in one of her moments when hysteria seemed about to explode from her perfectly coiffed, manicured, pedicured body. "I know my history. I know all about Marie Antoinette. They will just tell us to eat cake and then lop off our heads." She patted her hair as if to make certain it would look decent on the fall.

"This isn't the Bastille, Hill. They aren't going to take us to the guillotine." Jane's voice sounded tired in spite of her efforts to reassure Hillary.

"How do you know that? You admitted you don't know anything about Monacoan law."

"Trust me on this one, Hill."

"Trust you?" Hillary's voice was shrill. "I trusted you not to get us into this mess. The reason I hired you is to—"

"Wait a minute! Wait a minute! You've got to explain to me exactly how I was the one who got us into this. I don't recall inviting anyone to shoot at us or try to run us down on the autoroute. And I don't recall that I was the one who snuck us into the casino."

"Well I suppose you think it was my fault, when all I was trying to do was save our lives." Hillary sat down on the bottom bunk again, looking tired and defeated.

Jane hesitated a moment, then put her arm around Hillary's shoulders. "Listen to us at each other's throats, blaming each other. We're both just tired and scared."

Hillary turned her face to look at Jane. "Don't tell me you're scared, Jane. One of us has to be brave. It comes more naturally to you. That's why I hired you."

"It comes more naturally to me?"

"Well, sure, you're from California."

"Why didn't I see this coming?"

"Well, you're used to danger. You have to learn to be brave."

"I'm used to danger?"

Hillary sighed impatiently. "Well, of course. All those earthquakes. Charles Manson. Charlton Heston and the NRA." Hillary gave her a pleading look. "You'll think of something, won't you, Jane?"

Jane took a deep breath, thinking she might explain that living through a few tremors had only served to make her more scared, and that she'd had the good fortune to never meet either Charles Manson or Charlton Heston. In the end, all she said was, "Sure, Hill. I told you, I'll think of something."

For the next few hours, Hillary fretted while Jane chewed her fingernails, feeling helpless, unable to think of anything she could do to get them out of the mess they'd found themselves in. The only useful thing she did was to hold up the blanket they had pulled from the bed to shield Hillary as she used the toilet.

Finally, Jane, feeling completely exhausted, sank down onto the bed and was about to lie down, but Hillary startled her by crying out to her.

"Jane! Don't lie down on that thing! You don't know who's been there."

Jane sat up, gave the bed a suspicious glance, and stood to join Hillary pacing the floor. They were both distracted by the sudden appearance of an attendant who approached their cell. He stopped, gave each of them a cursory glance, and then spoke to them in French for several seconds, using his hands to punctuate and embellish everything he said. Then he turned and walked away.

Hillary grabbed Jane's arm, eager with anticipation. "What did he say?"

"How should I know?"

"Jane! Don't fail me now. I'm sure you can translate what he said if you just think about it."

"OK, it was something about your grandmother and all the Kappas from the University of Alabama. They're going to spring us."

Hillary looked at Jane in silence for a long moment and then turned away, sniffling.

"Ah, Hill, I'm sorry. You're right, I get a little rough around the edges when I'm scared."

Hillary turned around, drying her eyes daintily with the tips of her fingers. "So you admit it. You are scared."

"Maybe a little." She saw the look on Hillary's face and added quickly, "Hey, we've been in tight spots before, haven't we? I mean, they can't keep us forever, can they? Somebody is going to start looking for us eventually."

Hillary seemed cheered by that, although she had reached for Jane's hand when she sat down next to her on the bottom bunk. She was still holding it tightly when the guard returned with a tray on which were placed two bowls of something that looked like soup and a baguette.

They both ate the soup and bread eagerly, since they hadn't eaten since they'd left Lenoir, and it was now well into the evening. After the first two or three bites, Hillary put down her spoon and looked at Jane.

"You would think in a country known for its cuisine they would use fresh vegetables, wouldn't you? These potatoes have been frozen, and any chef worth his salt knows what that does to a potato." After her pronouncement, she picked up her spoon again and finished the soup.

The guard came to pick up the tray, and Hillary called to his indifferent back as he walked away, "The right herbs can do wonders to plain fare. A little rosemary and thyme would give it a fresher taste."

When she turned around, the worried, harried look had intensified in her eyes. She sighed heavily and went back to the bunk. In a little while, weariness had overcome her to the point that she lay down on the offensive mattress, lying on her back with an arm covering her eyes.

Jane crawled up to the top bunk and was soon listening to Hillary's soft snore. Within a few moments, she, too, was asleep.

The first light of morning had just begun to crawl through the bars of the window when a noise, like rain hitting the window, startled Jane awake. She glanced out the window but saw nothing at first. She heard the noise again, and realized it wasn't rain but pebbles hitting the window. She walked closer and stood on her tiptoes, trying to peer outside, but the window was too high.

In the next moment, she saw Buddy's face peering at her upside down through the bars on the window.

Jane sucked in her breath, and the sound startled Hillary awake. She sat up quickly.

"What was that?" Hillary asked, getting up to stand next to Jane.

"It was Buddy!"

"Buddy? Are you sure?" Hillary's voice was hoarse with sleep.

Before Jane could answer, Buddy's face appeared again. This time, he was holding up a piece of paper on which he had scrawled the words, "I am going to bust you out."

"Oh Lord!" Hillary said. "Do you suppose he can?"

"This is crazy," Jane said.

"How will he do it? We'll have to be on the lam, won't we? Like Thelma and Louise."

"We're not going to be on the lam. We're going to ask for a lawyer and an interpreter. We're going to speak to someone from the American Consulate. We are not going to depend upon Buddy Fletcher."

"But, Jane, you know what they say: A bird in hand . . ."

"No!" Jane was pacing the floor, worried that Buddy really might try something that would get them in even more trouble.

"How would he do it?" Hillary was excited now, no longer depressed.

"I don't know. Buddy's good at breaking into places, but breaking into a jail would go against his principles, I should think. It's more like him to bust out."

"How did he find us?" Hillary was stretching to try to see out the window. "Buddy of all people! I thought it would be Billy who found us."

Buddy's appearance had given Jane a flicker of hope, in spite of her protests. At least someone knew where they were. She paced the floor, wishing she could talk to Buddy. "If Buddy's here, I wonder where the girls are. Where Beau is."

Hillary glanced at the window. "Why doesn't he come back? Why doesn't Billy come to rescue us?" She sank down to the bunk again, lay down, and covered her eyes with her hand.

She was still lying in that position an hour later, and Jane was still staring at the window, hoping, in spite of herself, for Buddy to appear again, when the sound of automatic prison doors sliding open snapped her head around. A guard they'd not seen before walked up to their cell.

"Here," he said in English. He unlocked the cell, pushed the door back, and stood aside.

Hillary sprang to her feet and at the same moment Beau appeared beside the guard.

"Beau!" Jane was surprised at the instinct that led her to throw her arms around him. She pulled away. "Listen, Beau, we are in deep trouble. They think we were trying to rob the casino. Can you get us a lawyer? We'll need to—"

"You won't need a lawyer," Beau said.

"Of course we will. We can't—"

"You are free to go, madame," the English-speaking guard said. "I'm afraid there has been a mistake."

"Of course there's been a mistake." Hillary was becoming her old indignant self again.

Jane grabbed her hand. "Let it go, Hillary. We're free. No point in complicating things." She turned to Beau. "Where are the girls? Are they all right?"

"They're fine. They're with Billy."

"With Billy? You found him?" Hillary sounded excited.

Beau nodded. "Actually, he found us. He thought you had forgotten to pick him up, so he rented a car and drove to Lenoir. Then, when he learned you'd gone to meet him, he got a little worried."

"This way," the guard said, leading them to the waiting room so they could retrieve their belongings.

"Oh, I can just see him!" Hillary said. "He has this way of chewing his lip when he gets worried."

Beau laughed. "He did more than chew his lip. He drove into Lenoir and made a few phone calls until he found out what had happened. I suggested he start with the police department. Took him a while to find someone who spoke English, but once he found them, it didn't take long to find out what had happened. So then Billy made some more calls and apparently saved your skins. I don't know how he did it."

"Oh, Billy has connections," Hillary said.

"But why didn't he come himself?" Jane asked. "And why was Buddy out there hanging on a ledge telling us he was going to bust us out?"

Beau shook his head. "Buddy got impatient when I ran into a little red tape in the front office here. He got himself up on that ledge so you'd know help had come. Like to got himself arrested, but I got him down. He's safe in the car now."

"And Billy," Jane said. "You still haven't told us why he didn't come himself."

"Oh, he's here, all right," Beau said, "but someone had to wait in the lobby with the girls, and those two were having so much fun with him, they insisted that he be the one to stay. He's waiting for the two of you now."

12

The *préfet de police,* a rotund man with heavy jowls and graying temples, leaned forward from where he was seated behind his desk. He appeared eager to speak with Jane and Hillary. They had been allowed to change out of their prison clothes and had their belongings returned to them, including Hillary's casino winnings, which the *préfet* had converted to cash.

"Ah, mesdames, please allow me to apologize. There was a terrible—how do you say—misunderstanding. We had been tipped, as you say in your country, that someone was going to attempt to rob the casino, and the manager and the guard thought your actions were suspicious. As you were told, we had been watching you since the French police notified us of your high speed on the autoroute. We thought then you were escaping from another robbery."

"Suspicious?" Hillary was indignant. "You call our behavior suspicious when we were only trying to save our own lives?"

"Ah yes, you were being pursued, you said earlier." The *préfet* leaned forward even more. "Tell me about the man you say was pursuing you on the autoroute." His English, though heavily accented by his mother tongue, was understandable. Jane assumed the considerable number of English-speaking tourists who visited the tiny principality made that a necessity.

"Well, it was just awful!" Hillary spoke in her breathless, throaty voice. "I mean, I didn't know what to do! They were shooting at us, can you imagine?"

The *préfet*'s eyebrows came up. "Shooting?"

"Yes," Jane and Hillary said at the same time.

"Why would anyone want to shoot at you?"

Jane shook her head and was about to confess that she had no idea, but Hillary had a ready answer. "It was pretty obvious that they were shooting at us because they wanted to kill us."

"Mais oui!" The *préfet* leaned back in his chair. "There is some reason someone would want to kill you?"

Hillary spoke in a voice filled with indignation. "I tell you what, I think they just don't like people from Prosper, Alabama, around here. There have been two people from Prosper killed already, and we're not that big a town, so you can imagine what it will do to the population if this keeps up. I have to warn you, it's going to give y'all a bad reputation in Alabama if y'all insist on killing us."

The *préfet* smiled a little condescendingly. "I can assure you, madame, that the Principality of Monaco has nothing against you, and I am not aware of anyone from Alabama being killed here."

"Well, maybe not." Hillary stood and walked to one of the long windows to the left of the *préfet*'s desk. She appeared to be measuring them with her eye. "But those men followed us here all the way from Lenoir." She turned around to face the *préfet*. "They could have killed us, you know."

"Can you describe these men? Were they, perhaps, someone you know?"

Jane tried to speak, but Hillary interrupted her.

"Someone I know? I should hope not! I don't associate with that kind of person." Hillary sat in her chair again and leaned toward the *préfet*. "One of them had on a brown suit with a gray tie." There was a note of shock in her voice.

"Mon dieu!" the *préfet* said and raised his eyebrows again.

Jane was finally able to speak. "We couldn't see them very well when they were in the car, and then in the casino, we saw them only briefly, and they were wearing masks."

"Masks?" The *préfet* seemed puzzled.

"Halloween masks. Like children wear. You know, the rubber kind that sort of looks like real people."

"Mmmm," the *préfet* said.

Hillary glanced at her watch.

"You are in a hurry?" the *préfet* asked, noticing Hillary.

"My husband is waiting for me outside. I haven't seen him in several days, and I was just hoping I could—"

The *préfet* brightened. "Your husband? Monsieur Scarborough? But of course, you must not keep him waiting." He stood and opened the door for her. Jane started to leave as well, but the *préfet* stopped her.

"Un moment, s'il vous plaît. It will only be a few minutes. I have some more questions."

"But my daughter is—"

"Only a few minutes."

Jane hesitated and watched Hillary moving away with her finishing school walk, her high heels clicking on the hard tile floor. Then Jane turned, with reluctance, back into the office.

The *préfet*'s questions were routine. Were there any more details she could give him as to the description of the men? Could she describe the car? Would she describe exactly what happened? Where were they staying in France? Were there more details she could supply about the two dead men Madame Scarborough had mentioned?

Jane gave him all the information she could, including the names of the two dead men from Prosper, where their bodies were found and when, about the strange notes left at the château with the Knights Templar symbol, the fact that Guillaume Daudet, the owner of winery in Lenoir, had been arrested for their murder, and she gave him the supposed motive.

The *préfet* wrote furiously while she talked, but his only comment was, "Ah yes, the Mas du Compte in Lenoir. I know it well. Small winery. Excellent wine." He tapped his pen on the desk with a pensive look on his face, his lips slightly pursed. "You say Monsieur Vautrin of the police department in Lenoir is investigating this? And he has made the arrest?"

Jane nodded, and the *préfet* tapped his pen a moment longer.

"You will be in Lenoir long?"

"Another ten days."

The *préfet* nodded, tapped some more. *"Très bien,"* he said at length. "Forgive me for keeping you this long time. You have been very helpful, as I hoped you would. Madame Scarborough is—how do you say—very excitable. It makes her difficult to understand."

Jane stood up, started to leave.

"You must be very careful, madame." The look in the *préfet*'s eyes, his tone of voice, was frightening to Jane.

"Yes, of course I will."

"No, I mean *very* careful, madame. Your life could be in danger."

"You mean those men who were chasing us? Do you know who they are? What they want?" Jane's voice shook.

A rigid veil of professionalism fell across the *préfet*'s face. "I do not know who they are or what they want, but I believe they were after you. I am warning you to be careful, that is all."

"I'll remember to do that." Jane hurried out of the room, suddenly possessed with an even more urgent need to see Sarah.

When she got to the front lobby, it was not Sarah who greeted her, however, but Beau Jackson.

Jane's eyes searched the room. "Where are the others? Where's Sarah?"

Beau took her arm, led her toward the door. "They left early in the van because the girls didn't want to miss the parade in Lenoir."

"Parade?"

"Some sort of local festival. The girls learned about it from Madame Hulot when she stopped by. We were all worried sick about what might have happened to you." He moved his arm to her waist as he helped her across a busy street to the Citroën Hillary had rented. "Everyone, that is, except Sarah and Shakura. Billy Scarborough did a good job of distracting and reassuring them. He's pretty good at magic tricks, you know. Does it for the Shriners back home in Prosper all the time."

"He's pretty good at a disappearing act, that's for sure."

"At what?"

"Never mind. Are you sure Sarah's all right?"

"She's fine. Buddy watches over her like a mother hen."

"He does it for 'ol' Jim Ed,' you know."

Beau shrugged slightly. "Maybe, but I think he's genuinely fond of Sarah and you, too." He looked at her, studying her face. "Hey, don't feel so bad about Sarah going back with the others. She was really torn about staying here, but once Hillary convinced her you were all right, she couldn't resist going back with Shakura to see that parade. She's only ten."

Jane sighed heavily and leaned her head back on the seat of the car. "I know. It's just that after a brush with danger, I have this instinctive need to gather my young under my wing."

"I want to know more about those men Hillary said were chasing you." Beau looked at her, that professional frown creasing his forehead. "I trust you told the policeman in there about them."

"Of course."

"And what did he say?"

"He said to be careful."

"Is that all?"

"That's all," Jane said, then added, "I think he knows who they are."

Beau jerked his head toward her suddenly. "Why do you think that?"

Jane shook her head. "I don't know. It's just a hunch. Nothing concrete."

Beau's frown had deepened. "Damn. I wish I could have gone in there with you, but they wouldn't let me. I tried to tell them I'm a cop, but no one spoke English well enough to understand."

"This is getting too scary, Beau. I'm ready to take my daughter and Shakura back home to Prosper where the biggest danger is the weather. An Alabama tornado seems like a picnic compared to this."

Beau looked at her. "I'll take you back tomorrow if that's what you want."

Jane smiled at his sudden show of male protectivness and found she liked it. Maybe too much, she thought. She couldn't afford to turn into a Southern belle in need of protection. She had a daughter to raise and a life to make for herself. On her own.

Beau hadn't seen her smile. He was frowning at the road. "Before we leave, whenever we leave, I think we should go to Vautrin first and tell him about the men who took a shot at you. I have a feeling, just like you, that there's some connection to the murders. Vautrin needs to know. Maybe he'll have some insight."

"Will we have time to see him as soon as we get back?"

Beau nodded. "We should."

"I'm really serious about wanting to get this over with and get my daughter out of danger."

"Don't worry," Beau said. "I'm going to protect you."

Jane smiled again and leaned her head back on the seat,

allowing herself to feel, for the moment at least, secure. Within a few minutes, she was asleep, exhausted from a restless night in jail.

She awoke just as Beau reached the street paralleling the Rhône that put them in Lenoir. As they passed the outer reaches and were headed toward the town proper, Jane sensed the excitement. When they drew closer, Jane could see that the town was alive with activity, and the people-filled streets appeared to writhe like so many tentacles.

"We'll never find the girls in that crowd," Jane said, her voice filled with dismay.

"We'll find them." Beau sounded more grim than confident. "And Vautrin, too," he added. He got out of the car, then opened the door for Jane and led her into the crowd.

"What's the celebration all about?" Jane asked, clinging to Beau's hand as he pulled her through the crush of bodies.

Beau had to shout to be heard over the raucous merriment of the crowd. "Has something to do with the history of the town. Something to do with the old castle being saved from the Saracens. Maybe nobody remembers for sure. Just an excuse for a celebration."

"There's Vautrin over there!" Jane had spotted him at the intersection of two of the narrow streets. He was shoving his way through the crowd, moving away from them.

Beau shouted his name to get his attention, but his words were lost in the crashing tide of merriment. In the next moment, Jane heard her name being called, that distinct almost two-syllable pronunciation that could only come from Hillary.

Jane saw her waving from across the street. "Jane! I'm over here, lamb!"

Jane waved back and moved toward her, hoping the girls were with her, but Hillary appeared to be alone. Jane pushed her way through the crowd toward Hillary. Somewhere behind her, she heard Beau calling.

"Jane, wait a minute! Don't get lost in this mess."

When she turned around, she didn't see him. She called his name once, then pushed her way toward Hillary again.

Hillary reached a hand out when Jane was close enough and pulled. "Oh, lamb, I'm so glad I found you. I got lost from Billy and Buddy and the girls somehow."

"Are the girls all right? Is Sarah—"

"Oh yes, the girls are fine. They're real excited about the parade." Hillary glanced up and down the street. "It ought to start just any minute now."

Indeed, at that second, they heard horns, trombones and clarinets, spewing out a confetti of sound, and along with it, the underlying primitive heartbeat of a drum lulling the crowd to a hush. The music grew louder, and Jane could see, down the street, the top of a banner waving in the breeze.

Jane and Hillary were standing on the narrow sidewalk of the Rue de Château, the one-street business district of Lenoir, and the widest street in the tiny village of narrow warrens. The crowd had parted to allow the parade to pass.

The banner bearer in the front of the parade was a middle-aged man dressed in a cheap suit but looking, nevertheless, dignified. He was undoubtedly the mayor or some important city official, Jane thought.

He was followed by a group of men and women walking in costumes, some in animal skins to represent the earliest invaders of the area, and some in the simple cloaks and hats of peasants. It was a hodgepodge of history that walked by them, Roman soldiers interspersed with women dressed in the empire-waist gowns of the Napoleonic era and one, even, in a frilled collar of the sixteenth century. There was a man dressed as Charlemagne, several as troubadours singing their poetry in what Jane thought might have been the Languedoc dialect, and a fierce-looking warrior in a shaggy wig, an ugly mask, and a fake animal skin.

There was a tonsured monk, and a man wearing a medieval helmet and carrying a broad banner on which had been painted the Templars' cross. Some of the men carried staffs and clubs, the weapons of their early history, and some of the women carried scythes and pitchforks, looking as if they'd stepped out of a Van Gogh painting.

The representatives of the town's history swirled and fused with no clear lines to separate one era from another, blurring Jane's sense of time and her sense of what seemed now to be its artificial demarcations. The whole effect was dizzying.

The unruly mass was followed by the band, still playing its brassy, splashy river of notes backed up by the throbbing drum. After them came children and adults as well with their pets: dogs and cats festooned with ribbons and flowers.

Hillary leaned close to Jane and spoke. "I don't know how I got lost from Billy and the girls. They were right behind me, and when I turned around, they were gone."

"What about Buddy?" Jane had an uncomfortable feeling. She'd known Buddy more than once to take advantage of a situation that distracted everyone.

Hillary shook her head as if to say she didn't know what had happened to Buddy. "And Beau? Didn't I see you with him just a minute ago?"

Jane glanced all around, looking for Beau again.

Hillary's face was pinched with worry. "Oh dear. I just hope they all show up at the château."

"I want to find them before then," Jane said. "I want to make sure the girls are safe." Her eyes searched the crowd, looking for some sign of her blond daughter and her dark-skinned friend, but they were nowhere in sight.

Hillary leaned toward her again. "Where do you suppose Beau went?"

"To find Vautrin." Jane leaned close to Hillary to make sure she could hear her over the low rumble of the parade and the crowd. "He wants to tell him about the men who followed us and shot at us. He thinks there may be some connection to the murders."

"Some of Daudet's henchmen?"

"Maybe. But I still don't think Daudet did it. And where did you get that term *henchmen,* Hillary?"

"Since I met you, I've made several forays into the dark side of life. You pick up things." While Hillary was speaking, she was studying the parade participants, who, now that they had reached the end of the business district, had begun to mingle with the spectators.

Jane rolled her eyes. "Well, I'm glad I've helped further your education."

Hillary grabbed Jane's arm. "Look! Over there! Isn't that Madame Hulot?" She pointed to a woman dressed as Marie Antoinette might have looked, in a gown cinched tightly at the waist, with ruffled sleeves and a low, ruffled neckline, and an elaborate headdress.

Hillary waved and called to her. Madame Hulot saw her and waved back, agitated. She appeared to be trying to say something to them. Before Jane could determine what she was saying, however, she was distracted by a figure looming behind Hillary. It was the man in the knight's helmet. It still covered his face, and he now carried the banner with the Maltese cross folded under his arm.

Without knowing why, Jane grabbed Hillary's hand and pulled her roughly toward her.

"Good Lord, Jane, what are you doing?" Hillary followed along reluctantly, trying to avoid bumping into people as Jane pulled her onward. She stopped after they'd gone a few yards and looked behind them.

Hillary was preoccupied. "Now my hair is a mess, Jane." She sounded a little petulant, and she tried to pat her hair back in place.

Jane's eyes were still on the knight. "Don't worry about your hair, Hillary. I think we're being followed again."

"Again?" Hillary had lost her preoccupation and now sounded alarmed. "Is it the same men we saw on the autoroute?"

"I'm not sure." Jane saw, over her shoulder, the man

pushing his way through the crowd, moving toward them, carrying a pitchfork.

With Jane in the lead, they forced their way through the crowd with ruthlessness fueled by fear and Jane's instinct to search out Sarah when danger was near. Every time she looked back, though, the man was following.

Hillary had seen the man as well. "Who is that?" She was breathless, still clinging to Jane's hand.

They stopped for a moment, and Jane searched the crowd, thinking they had lost him. "A knight," she said, and pulled Hillary along again when she spotted him.

"A Knight Templar, you mean?"

Jane didn't respond. They had reached a relatively deserted street by now, and she ran faster, pulling Hillary after her. Hillary seemed to be holding back more and more. Finally she came to a stop, breathing hard, her coral-tipped fingers lying across her chest.

"I just can't do this anymore," Hillary said, puffing. "It's not good for my skin to get it all sweaty like this."

"For Christ's sake, Hillary, forget about your—" Jane lost her voice when she saw the knight suddenly round a corner of the narrow street, only a few feet from them. He still carried the pitchfork, and he was headed straight for the two of them. Jane felt frozen to the spot, unable to move, and Hillary, clinging to her arm, appeared equally immobilized.

Hillary regained her senses enough to scream, and in the same instant, a long staff protruded from around the corner and hit the knight hard on the head. The blow made his helmet ring like a warning bell. The staff struck again. The man fell to the ground, and Marie Antoinnete emerged from behind the building.

13

Madame Hulot's Marie Antoinnette wig slid forward as she leaned over the prone figure on the ground. She poked at the visor on the man's helmet with the staff she'd used as a weapon. The visor flipped open.

"Ah!" she said in what could have been both disgust and surprise when she saw the face behind the visor. *"C'est* Louis Gustave!" She pushed at her wig, setting it even more askew, and glanced at Jane and Hillary. "I know this man," she said, gesturing wildly with the staff and her free hand. "It is Louis, who works for me in my garden sometimes." She frowned and shook her head, which sent her wig yet another interesting angle. "But he is no good. *Très paresseux!* Very lazy, and"—she leaned toward them and pointed a finger to her head—"a little slow with the wits."

Hillary glanced at the man with wariness. "But why in the world would he be chasing Jane and me?"

Madame Hulot shrugged and shook her head. *"Je ne sais pas.* Who knows? But I tried to warn you. I hear him, you see. I hear him talking to someone saying, 'I will get the two American women.' He was—what do you call it?

Bragging? Yes, he was bragging and saying to one of his no-good friends, 'I will get the American women.' "

Jane shook her head, puzzled. "But why?"

"Why?" Madame Hulot's face was animated with expression, and her hands punctuated everything she said. "Why, you say? For money, that is why!"

"Well, my Lord! That just doesn't make sense," Hillary said. "Why would anyone pay to harm me? I don't know about you, Jane, but I have never done anything to upset anyone that bad in all of my life."

Jane opened her mouth, about to protest the implication that it was her fault and to point out there had been several times Hillary had upset a number of people, including Jane herself, enough to want to throttle her. But she resisted the temptation and turned to Madame Hulot instead. "Do you have any idea who might have paid Louis to come after us?"

Madame Hulot shook her head and shrugged at the same time. "Do I have the ideas? All I know is that the world is full of the evil. And as for the ideas, I can only think of the ideas for my cooking school with no time to try to understand the evil in the world. And that reminds me, why were you not in class this morning, Madame Scarborough?" She shook a finger at Hillary. "You cannot become a master of *la grande cuisine* if you do not attend all of my classes. You missed the *poulet en cocote,* so now all you have is the beef and the fish. Life is not complete unless you know how to cook *le poulet* as well. *Mon dieu!* What can I say!"

"Well!" Hillary said in a huff. "I couldn't very well be in your class when I was in ... Well, when I was indisposed."

"Indisposed!" Madame Hulot's huff was equal to Hillary's. "What does this mean, this indisposed? Are my classes not important enough to—"

Jane interrupted. "What Hillary was trying to say is that we were in jail."

Madame Hulot's eyes widened. "Jail? *Mon dieu!* For what reason?"

"It's a long story," Jane said. "The short version is that we were mistaken for thieves, but before we got to that point, someone tried to run us down on the autoroute and even tried to kill us."

Madame Hulot shook her head. "But this is so strange. People trying to kill you. You are some kind of American gangster, perhaps?"

One of Hillary's hands went to her chest in a gesture of alarm. "You're asking me? I should say not! Why, I've never even *seen* one. Why, I'm a—"

"I was just wondering," Jane said, hoping to stave off Hillary using her grandmother's lineage and her past affiliation with the Junior League and her sorority as a defense, "if Louis here could have been one of the guys chasing us in Monte Carlo yesterday."

Madame Hulot shook her head, and a concerned frown crept across her forehead. "Someone chasing you? Strange indeed. But it could not have been Louis. He was in my garden all day. Such a lazy man! He got only half the work done."

"Then who?" Jane said, as much to herself as to anyone.

Madame Hulot sighed and shook her head again. "I do not know. It is so strange, all this evil that has come to Lenoir. Two Americans dead as well as poor little Eugenie, and Guillaume Daudet accused of killing them! And now someone is trying to kill you. It is too much! Too much!" She spread her hands in a gesture of despair.

Jane glanced at Louis. "If he ever wakes up, we could ask him."

Hillary took a step away from Louis. "I don't want to be around when he wakes up. The man's dangerous!" Just as she spoke, Louis groaned and stirred slightly. Hillary gasped and almost knocked Jane down, trying to move even farther away from him.

"At least he's not dead," Jane said. "I was beginning to

worry we might get stuck with a murder rap."

"Good Lord, Jane!" Hillary sounded both alarmed and frightened. "You come up with the most gruesome things!"

Louis groaned again and opened his eyes, seeing Jane, who was bending over him. *"Vous!"* he said, pointing at her, and then mumbled something in French. Madame Hulot leaned close to hear him.

"What did he say?" Jane asked, leaning over him as well.

"Lord, Jane, don't ask." Hillary was trying to pull her away.

Madame Hulot straightened her back and pushed back her wig. "He said you are the ones he was supposed to kill."

Hillary pulled harder at Jane's arm. "I told you not to ask."

At the same time Jane said, "Ask him who paid him to kill us."

Madame Hulot leaned over Louis again and spoke to him in French, but there was no answer. Not even when she prodded him with the staff. She looked at Jane and Hillary and shrugged.

Jane felt her spine grow tense. "Christ! He's not dead, is he?"

"Oh no, he is not dead." Madame Hulot pointed, with the staff, to the rise and fall of his chest.

"I want to get out of here," Jane said. "This is all too scary. I want to go find my daughter." She glanced at Louis, whose eyelids had begun to flutter a little. "But we ought to get that man to a doctor. And we ought to tell Vautrin what he said about wanting to kill us."

"Ah!" Madame threw up her hands, including the one that held the staff, which bumped her wig and knocked it in yet another direction. "I will take care of Louis. I will tell Vautrin. You go find your daughter. It is important to protect the children. I know, after all, am I not a mother myself? Ah yes, and a very good one at that. Both of my sons have good positions with the government, you know.

Both very important, of course. But not so well fed, now that they are married. Ah, what can I say? No one prepares food like Madame Hulot!" She had pulled a cellular phone from somewhere in the folds of her eighteenth-century-style gown and dialed numbers as she spoke. "I call the ambulance," she said glancing at Jane and Hillary. "Go! Go!" She used the staff to shoo them away. "I will take care of Louis."

Jane gave Madame Hulot a wave and turned back toward the Rue de Château. "Come on, Hillary, I want to find the girls."

"And I want to find Billy," Hillary said, following close behind.

The street was full of people again, now that the parade had ended, but the crowd was noticeably more sparse than it had been before the parade.

"I don't see them." Hillary was standing on her toes, scanning the crowd.

"Maybe they went into one of the restaurants for a drink or a snack," Jane offered.

They searched all of the pastry shops and restaurants on the short street, but saw no sign of either Billy or the girls, or of Beau or Buddy. As they left the last shop, the crowd had dwindled even more, and Jane saw the unmistakable solid torso of Beau Jackson standing on the opposite side of the street, scanning the crowd as if he was looking for someone.

"Beau!" She waved her hand as she called to him.

"There's Buddy, too," Hillary said, as Buddy approached Beau, shaking his head.

Beau's eyes seemed to light up when he saw the two of them, and he hurried across the street, followed by Buddy.

Everyone spoke at once.

"Where the hell y'all been?" Buddy said.

"We've been searching everywhere for you," Beau said at the same time.

"Where are the girls?" Jane asked.

"Have y'all seen Billy?" Hillary asked.

"The girls are with Billy." Beau's authoritative cop's voice overrode everyone else's.

"Where's Billy?" Jane and Hillary said together.

"Good God, Miz Ferguson," Buddy said, shaking his head, "I wish you wouldn't keep slipping out of my sight like that."

"Where are Billy and the girls?" There was desperation and anxiety in Jane's voice.

Beau put a comforting arm around her shoulders. "The girls got tired, so Billy took them back to the château. I told him I'd find you two and tell you where they were so you wouldn't worry and be looking for them." He turned his gaze to Hillary. "Billy said to tell you he'll see you at the château."

Hillary was checking her makeup in a palm-sized mirror she'd pulled from her purse.

In spite of Beau's reassurance, Jane still was not entirely comforted. The frightening events of the last two days had left her feeling insecure, and she wouldn't be at ease until she could hold both of the girls in her arms.

Jane looked up at Beau, who was walking beside her, still with his arm around her. "Did you find Vautrin? Did you tell him about the men who followed us and took a shot at us?"

She saw Beau's frown reappear on his brow. "I saw him, but not until after the parade ended, and he was busy controlling the crowd. There wasn't much time to talk."

"But you did tell him about the two guys who followed us." The memory of them made Jane even more tense.

"I told him, but he seemed to think it was just pranksters. Kids maybe, out for a dangerous joy ride, trying to scare drivers."

Hillary hesitated and turned to Beau before she got into the car. "It wasn't pranksters. I hope you told him that, Beau Jackson. Those men were serious. We saw them in the casino, and they weren't kids. It was somebody shooting at us!"

"She's right," Jane said. "It was like they were stalking us."

"There's even more now!" Hillary glanced at Jane as if for confirmation. "A man tried to kill us with a pitchfork."

"What?" Beau said.

"What you say?" Buddy said at the same time.

Jane breathed a deep sigh. "Yes. Madame Hulot said it was some poor half-wit who does gardening for her."

Beau's frown was back. "Do you think there's a connection to the men who were chasing you?"

Jane shook her head. "Who knows. I don't understand anything that's happening."

"We've *got* to tell that policeman about all this," Hillary said.

Buddy was shifting nervously on his feet, and his face had reddened. "Policeman, hell. I got to take care of this myself."

"Buddy! Don't you dare," Jane said.

Beau put a hand on Buddy's shoulder. "Vautrin said we'd talk about all this tomorrow. He said to come by his office. We'll tell him about this latest incident, too. Now is not the time to take things into your own hands, Buddy." It was hard for Jane to read Beau's expression, but his frown was still there, and a muscle twitched in his jaw. There was something in his eyes, too, something dark and worried.

When they reached the car, Jane hesitated long enough that Buddy usurped the front seat that Beau obviously had meant for her. She slid in beside Hillary in the back. Beau breathed a resigned sigh and got in the driver's side next to Buddy.

Buddy promptly turned around in the seat to grill Jane. "How'd they treat you in jail, Miz Ferguson? They didn't give you no shit, did they?"

"They didn't give me no shit, Buddy. Everything was lovely."

" 'Cause if they did, I could take care of 'em for you. Course, I don't have the connections over here that I do at home, but I could manage." He glanced quickly at Beau. "It ain't that I'd ever do anything illegal, even at home, you understand."

"Yeah, sure, Buddy," Beau said, without taking his eyes off the road.

"I mean it, Miz Ferguson. You just let me know, and—"

"I said everything was just lovely, Buddy."

"No need for us to tell ol' Jim Ed about this."

"No need at all," Jane said.

"It'd just worry him." Buddy looked anxious.

"It'd just worry him." Jane added a derisive "Ha!"

Buddy didn't seem to notice. He was busy explaining an elaborate plan he'd worked out whereby Jane would not be out of his sight from now until she was safely back in Prosper.

Jane sighed heavily, feeling a headache coming on. She leaned against the back of the car and closed her eyes. She must have slept without realizing it, because it seemed that it was only the next second that they were on the driveway leading up to the château. Her head still hurt, and she still felt a taut bowstring of tension in her back.

She saw the van parked in the driveway and felt a little of the tightness in her spine relax. If the van was parked outside, that meant Billy and the girls were safe inside.

Jane called their names as soon as they stepped into the great hall. At the same time, Hillary was calling for Billy. The only answer, though, was the tomblike silence of the house.

When they had searched all the rooms and found no one, a troubled frown creased Hillary's forehead for a second, but she quickly brightened. "Why, they must be out at the stables, hon. You know how crazy the girls are about horses, and Billy knows a lot about them. He's always going off to Arkansas to the races."

Jane was out the door, hurrying to the stables, with the rest of the group following behind her. There was no sign of anyone except the horses, chewing the last of their hay. Even the stable boy had gone home for the day.

Jane felt a sinking feeling in her stomach, but she tried to ignore it. If the van was here, Billy and the girls had to be somewhere around.

"The winery maybe," Beau suggested.

"Yeah," Buddy said, "or that little ol' church. We ought to look there."

The winery was closed and securely locked, and the chapel was empty. When Jane emerged from the chapel, feeling even more uneasy, her fear escalated when she saw Buddy's face. It had gone white.

"If anything happens to them girls . . ." Tears welled in his eyes, and he turned away. The tears, Jane knew, were for Sarah and Shakura, and, for once, had nothing to do with how Jim Ed might react.

Even Hillary was subdued.

Beau put his arm around Jane's shoulders. "We'll find them," he said. "Don't worry."

Jane could hear the worry in his voice, in spite of his words. Still, Beau maintained his composure and came up with a plan for an organized search of the area with each person taking a different segment. They were to meet at the house in half an hour.

"By then, they'll probably be back there waiting for us anyway." There was a false brightness to Beau's voice.

But they weren't there waiting, and no one had seen them in the systematic search they made of the area.

Jane felt numb, too frightened and worried to speak or cry. Beau looked at her, his frown a deep furrow. "I'll take the van into the village and tell Vautrin." He placed his hand on Jane's shoulder. "You go inside and wait."

"I'm going with you." Jane was grateful that he had at least not told her to stop worrying.

"I'll go, too," Hillary said.

"No, please," Jane said. "Wait here. In case they show up."

Hillary nodded and reached to squeeze Jane's hand. "All right, dear. I'll cook dinner. The girls are sure to be hungry when they get back. I'll cook something they'll be sure to like. Stuffed niçoise tomatoes and a nice lemon soufflé." She had already started walking toward the kitchen.

Beau took Jane's arm and led her toward the door. "I don't want you to get your hopes up too much about the help we'll get from Vautrin," he said. "Most police departments don't even start a search until the party's been missing twenty-four hours."

Jane shook her head, unable to accept that no one would search for her daughter and her friend for a full day. "Surely, after all that has happened to us, he won't hesitate to look for them."

"Just try to take comfort in the fact that they're with Billy Scarborough. He's very resourceful." Beau was speaking in his professional tone of voice again, something he seemed to retreat to when things got difficult.

Beau had opened the front door for her, and they were about to leave when Buddy stopped them.

"I think you better take a look at this." He handed Beau a sheet of paper. "I found it over yonder by the window. I reckon the wind must of blew it off that table there. I think we was supposed to see it when we first come in the door."

Jane moved closer to Beau to read what was written on the paper. It had obviously been typed on a computer and printed, perhaps on a laser printer, and as soon as Jane read the first few words, she felt her blood turn to ice water.

The note read:

"If you want your daughter and her friend back, stop your meddling and go home now. Take the first flight out of Avignon. The children will follow on the next flight. Otherwise, death!"

14

Jane was numb with fear and with the horror of what she had just read. She couldn't think, couldn't move. She shook her head and uttered one word, "No," as if denial would somehow bring the children back.

"Has anyone seen my . . ." Hillary came back into the room but stopped when she saw the look on the faces of the others. "What is it? Is something wrong?"

Beau showed her the note.

Hillary's face went white, and she was speechless for a moment. She turned to Jane. "Oh lamb!" Hillary encircled her in her arms, and they clung to each other for a moment.

The light-headed feeling that swept over Jane was almost comforting, and she might have succumbed to an old-fashioned swoon had not Beau grasped her arm in a grip so tight it hurt. "Jane, you've got to tell me everything you know. You've got to tell me what you've learned that is so dangerous for you."

"I don't know." Her voice was barely audible, even to her own ears.

It was the words Hillary spoke that pulled her back and helped her regain her balance.

"Look at this paper!" She had grabbed the note from Beau's hand and was studying it. "See that oily film around the edges? It's the same paper those awful notes from Eugenie were written on."

Beau took it back from her and examined it himself. "By God, you're right," he said, almost under his breath.

Hillary shook her head. "But how could that be? Eugenie is dead."

"Eugenie must have been a pawn, Hill," Jane said, gaining a little of her composure. "Somebody must have paid her to leave those notes and then killed her when she learned too much."

"But who?" Hillary's voice was choked with worry.

"When we find that out, we'll find Billy and the girls," Beau said. He was still holding tight to Jane's arm as if he was afraid she might yet faint.

"Buddy! Where are you going?" Jane called to him as he reached the front door. He turned around, and Jane saw that his face was chiseled with fear and anger.

"I'm going to get them girls. This town ain't that big. I'll find 'em somehow."

Jane made a move to go with him, but Beau pulled her back. "Wait a minute, Buddy," Beau said. "We've got to do this right. The first thing is to go to the police."

Jane looked at Beau and then at Buddy. Beau was probably right. The correct way to do it was to go to the police, but her instincts were to go with Buddy. To leave no stone unturned until she found her daughter and her daughter's friend.

"Hell, a person could waste all day going to the cops." A muscle tightened in Buddy's jaw as he spoke. "They're going to ask questions, fill out them damn forms, then maybe in a day or two they'll get around to lookin'. I ain't wasting any time. I'm going after Miz Ferguson's little girl."

"Wait, Buddy . . ." Before Beau could say more, Buddy was out the door. Jane tried once again to follow him, and once again, Beau pulled her back. She didn't seem to be able to think straight. Should she break away and go with Buddy or give in to Beau's cool logic? Her indecision set her course.

"We're going to the police," Beau said, as if he had decided for her. He grabbed Hillary's arm and guided them both to the van. Jane saw Buddy driving away in the Citroën just as they stepped outside. He was driving too fast, and his last words echoed in Jane's head. For once he had referred to Sarah as Miz Ferguson's daughter. Her own. Not Jim Ed's.

Jane felt the numbing fear returning, and she allowed herself to be guided to the van and helped inside. Hillary did not insist upon driving. She seemed to have gone equally numb.

This time when they went into the tiny police building, another officer in the front office stopped them before they got to Vautrin's office. He looked vaguely familiar to Jane, and she thought perhaps she had seen him in the parade dressed as a troubador.

He spoke to them in French. *"Vous êtes Américaines, n'est-ce pas? Vous êtes perdues dans notre petite ville?"*

The words, spoken so fast, were incomprehensible to Jane. Apparently they were to Beau as well. "We want to see Vautrin," he said.

The officer raised an eyebrow. "Vautrin?"

"Yeah. Right away. We want to report a crime." Beau's voice had become hard-edged. He started past the officer toward Vautrin's office. The officer stood up suddenly, overturning his chair, and blocked Beau's way, spitting out a long spiel of angry French. He grabbed Beau and seemed ready to shove him.

"Oh my Lord!" Hillary reached for Jane as if she felt protective of her now.

At the same moment, Vautrin emerged from his office. "Maurice! *C'est bien. Laisse entrer les Americaines."* He smiled and held out his hands in a welcoming gesture to the three of them.

"Come in please," he said in English. "I hope you have not come to me with the problem again. I hope it is to tell me how much you have enjoyed the celebration today. I have looked into the chase on the autoroute. Drunks. That is all. We will find them and arrest them, do not worry."

"Drunks?" Jane shook her head. "It couldn't have been just drunks. Someone was trying to kill us, and I think it's connected to all the other murders."

Vautrin shook his head. "Madame, Madame! I am afraid you have seen too much American TV. *LA Law, Miami Vice* . . ."

"I'll tell you one thing," Hillary said, still holding protectively to Jane. "You ought to teach that deputy of yours some manners."

Vautrin raised an eyebrow. "Maurice? Ah, you must forgive him. He is—how do you say? Excitable? He wants to be in the car, you know. Patrolling the streets? But, I cannot allow it." He leaned forward and spoke conspiratorially. "Poor Maurice is blind with colors."

Hillary looked puzzled for a moment, then, "Oh, you mean color-blind."

Vautrin laughed. "Yes. He cannot tell what color the traffic lights are, but I find use for him here."

Hillary nodded. "Oh, then that explains why he was wearing one blue sock and one brown."

"Why are we talking about socks?" Jane was suddenly agitated. "My daughter has been kidnapped!"

Vautrin raised both eyebrows. "What is this you say?"

Beau shoved the note at Vautrin, who read it quickly, then looked up at the three of them. "Y'all have got to get your detectives on this now!" Beau's tension and worry seemed to have intensified his accent. "This is pretty damned serious and dangerous business. It has something to do with all those murders and that car that chased these women on the autoroute. I'll be willing to bet that wasn't just drunks or kids."

Hillary leaned across Vautin's desk. "My husband has been kidnapped, too, and he's an important man. Maybe you know him? Billy Scarborough?"

Vautrin frowned and shook his head. "I'm afraid, madame, that I don't know your husband, but—"

"The lady's right," Beau said, interrupting. "Billy Scarborough is a prominent citizen of Prosper. Enough so that this could make the papers and turn into an international incident. Not to mention one of the little girls is Jim Ed Ferguson's daughter. Big Birmingham law firm? Atlanta connections? You said you knew him."

"I assure you, monieur, I understand the seriousness of this matter." Vautrin was frowning as he studied the paper. He laid it down on his desk and raised his eyes to speak to them again. "I assure you also that I will see to it that your loved ones are safely returned."

Beau's fists were clenched in his lap. "How can you—"

Jane interrupted him. "But what can we do? We can't just sit around and wait. This is my daughter who is missing. She means more to me than life itself, and her friend is just as important."

"What can you do?" Vautrin leveled his gaze at Jane. "I suggest that you do just as the kidnappers suggest."

"What?" The word came from Jane's throat in an anguished rush.

"I suggest you go home. It appears, does it not, that all the kidnappers want is for you to be, as you Americans say, out of the hair."

Jane stood up, agitated. "You must be crazy if you think I'm going to leave here when my daughter is in danger. I'm going to stay here and—"

"And I'm not leaving, either!" Hillary stood and linked her arm in Jane's.

Vautrin held up his hands as if to protect himself from their anguish. "Please, please, mesdames, I understand that you must feel upset, but you must let me handle this."

"Upset? Mister, you don't know the half of it." Jane's voice had risen several decibels.

"I don't think y'all want to see her when she's really upset," Hillary said.

"Please, please, mesdames," Vautrin said again, making downward movements with his hands as if he were gesturing for them to lower both their voices and their bodies.

Jane forced herself to sit down. She glanced at Beau. His hands were still clenched, and his frown now seemed a permanent deep ridge.

Vautrin picked up the note again. "Please, let us look at this calmly. Someone took your loved ones captive from the château while you were in Monte Carlo." He glanced at Beau. "I agree that it would seem likely it has something to do with the murders. But," he said, turning his gaze to encompass the three of them, "it appears that the three people captured have not been harmed, *n'est-ce pas?*"

Beau leaned forward. "Just because there is an indication that they'll be returned unharmed doesn't mean—"

"Of course," Vautrin said, interrupting him. "One can never be sure, but allow me to offer my theory. In the case of the other murders, there was no warning. They had to be done quickly, it seems. This time, there are no bodies. There is only a warning. I say it is best not to risk harm. Instead, to do as they say. Go home." He raised his hands again, quickly, in anticipation of Jane's and Hillary's protest. "I know, I know. You do not want to leave, but it is the best way to get your loved ones back, and we must be thinking, of course, of saving the lives, *n'est-ce pas?*"

Jane shook her head. "I thought policemen always said don't give in to the demands of kidnappers." She saw, out of the corner of her eye, that Beau was sitting rigid in his chair.

"C'est vrai," Vautrain said, "when the demand is for money. This is more simple. The demand is only that you leave. I say it is worth the try."

Beau spoke at last. "There is no real guarantee they'll be returned even if the demand is met."

Vautrin's brow wrinkled in a worried frown. "But there is the indication you will never see them again alive if you do not do as they say."

Vautrin's words brought a chill to Jane, along with a dizzying wave of nausea. She felt Hillary's hand grope for hers.

"You must, of course, leave me instructions to contact you," Vautrin said. "And I give you my assurance we will not have leaves upturned to solve this." He stood in a gesture of dismissal.

When Jane saw that Hillary and Beau had risen from their seats, she, too, stood up. She still felt disoriented, and a sense of helplessness had begun to overwhelm her.

"Oh, I almost forget," Vautrin called out as they moved toward the door. "Louis Gustave, the man who chased you with *la fourche?* He is in custody. He meant no harm. Just a poor crazy."

"What do you mean, he meant no harm?" Hillary said. "He said he was going to kill us."

Vautrin shook his head. "Just a poor crazy. I am sorry he frightened you."

Jane turned away from Vautrin and followed the others out. She supposed his words about Louis Gustave were meant to be of some comfort to her, but nothing at this point could possibly give her comfort, except to have Sarah and Shakura safe and back with her again.

As they walked through the front office, Maurice was standing near a copy machine with a feather duster and a can of spray wax in his hand. He glared at them then went back to his dusting, spraying a sticky web of the wax on the paper cutter before he gave it an angry swipe with his feather duster.

As they left the building, Jane began to tremble, and she felt tears running down her cheeks. Beau's arm went around her immediately, and Hillary reached for her hand.

"Oh lamb, I know it's just awful, but try to take comfort in the fact that Billy's with them. If anybody can get them out of this, it's Billy." Jane saw that her worried expression belied her words. "What are we going to do?" Hillary asked, turning to Beau.

Beau shook his head. "Maybe Vautrin's right, I don't know."

"He's *not* right!" Jane was surprised at the anger in her own voice. "I will not run away and wait for some criminal to decide the fate of my daughter!"

She saw the muscle tighten in Beau's jaw and his frown come back. He helped her and then Hillary into the car. "I'm taking you home," he said, starting the engine.

Jane jerked her head toward him. "And then what?"

"Maybe Buddy was right after all," Beau said, half under his breath.

"You mean . . ." For the first time, Jane felt some hope.

"I'm taking you home, and then I'm going to help him look."

"Oh no you're not!" Hillary said.

"No way," Jane said at the same time. "If you're going, I'm going."

"Jane . . ."

"Don't you dare tell me it's dangerous. I don't care how dangerous it is. I hope you can understand that."

Beau stared at her a moment, wordless, then drove out of the parking lot. He seemed to be deep in thought as he drove, and he spoke little.

"You're taking us home," Jane said as he headed out of town, toward the château.

"We'll sit down and talk about this," Beau said. "Decide what to do."

"We have to start tonight!" Jane's voice was choked with fear and despair. "We can't wait any longer. You know that, don't you?"

Beau didn't answer. He was staring straight ahead. When Jane turned her eyes to see what he was looking at, she saw the Citroën in a cloud of dust coming toward them on the driveway.

The tiny car stopped in front of them and Sarah and Shakura tumbled out. Buddy had a little trouble unfolding himself from the driver's seat.

"Mom!" Sarah called.

Within seconds, Jane's door was open, and she had both Sarah and Shakura in her arms. "Oh thank God! Oh Sarah! Shakura! Are you all right? Did they hurt you?" She held them both at arm's length to inspect them.

"We're fine, Mom. Nobody hurt us." Sarah clung to her mother.

"Buddy rescued us, and Uncle Billy went after the guy that got us," Shakura said.

Beau had gotten out of the car as well, and was now standing beside them. "Who got you? How?"

Hillary hurried to join them. "Where's Billy? He went after who?"

Buddy ambled over, rubbing his back. "I told him it wasn't no use, but he was madder than hell. Said he was going after that guy."

Beau turned to Buddy. "Going after who? Going where?"

Buddy pushed his cap back on his head. "Well, you see, it's like this—"

Jane stood up and hugged Buddy. "How'd you do it, Buddy? How did you find them?"

Buddy shrugged. "It wasn't nothing really, I just—"

"You should have seen him, Mom," Sarah said. "The way he broke into that building was something else."

Jane looked at Buddy with surprise. "You broke into a building?"

"Where? What building?" Beau asked.

"Buddy's something else!" Shakura said.

"Are you sure Billy's all right?" Hillary was doing a nervous dance, hugging the girls, then moving to Buddy and then to Jane to hug each of them.

"Wait a minute! Wait a minute!" Beau's voice rose

above everyone else's. "Everybody just be quiet for minute!" After there was silence, he spoke again. "Now, let's go into the house, and I want you girls to start from the beginning. I want to know everything that happened. Then I want to hear from you, Buddy. I'll talk to Billy when he shows up."

When they were inside, with the girls sitting close to Jane, they began their story.

"We were all outside, see. It was after the parade, and we were tired of just hanging around," Sarah began, "and so we came back here, and Uncle Billy was going to help us ride the horses."

Jane raised an eyebrow at her daughter. "Uncle Billy?"

"Yes, Mom. That's what he told us to call him."

"That's when the man came and surprised us," Shakura said. "It was so scary."

"What did he look like?" Beau asked. "Did you get a good look at him?"

Shakura shook her head. "That's what made it scary. He had on a mask. It was so weird. Like one of those guys in the parade."

"Yeah," Sarah said. "You know, the guys that were in animal skins and they had those masks with the long, shaggy hair?"

"The Saracens," Jane said.

"I don't know what they are called. I just know they were scary," Sarah said.

"Yeah," Shakura said.

Beau nodded at both of them. "Go on."

Sarah shivered slightly. "Well, me and Shakura saw him at kind of the same time, I guess, and we both screamed. Uncle Billy came running out of that little building. You know, the one where they keep the saddles and bridles."

"Yeah, and he started yelling at the scary guy," Shakura said, "but the guy had a gun, and it was pointed at us, and he told Uncle Billy to shut up."

"He said shut up? He spoke English?" Beau asked.

Sarah and Shakura looked at each other. "Sort of," Sarah said.

Beau leaned closer. "What do you mean, sort of?"

"Well, he spoke to us in French sometimes, and when he did speak English, it was with that accent they have here," Sarah said.

Beau nodded. "So he was French."

Sarah shrugged. "I guess so."

"All right, go on," Beau urged. "What happened next?"

"He made us get in the car," Sarah said. "Me and Shakura in the front and Uncle Billy in the back, and—"

"What kind of car?" Beau interrupted.

"Black," Sarah said.

Shakura nodded. "With gray seats."

"You don't know the kind of car it was?" Beau asked.

Again Sarah and Shakura looked at each other uncertainly. "I think it was maybe a French car," Sarah said.

"A Citroën?" Beau asked.

"It was spelled R-e-n-a-u-l-t, I think," Shakura said. "I saw the name on the front."

"The same car that chased us on the autoroute!" Hillary said.

"Go on," Beau said to the girls.

Sarah took a deep breath. "Well, I think the man was afraid Uncle Billy would try to make him stop driving because he put his gun up close to my head, and he said something none of us could understand, but we got the idea."

"Oh my God!" Jane pulled Sarah close and hugged her again.

"Then we got to this building. It was like an apartment building, only real old, you know," Shakura said. "And he made us go upstairs."

"Yeah," Sarah said. "And then he tied us with some ropes, and he kept telling us in English that we had better not cause him any trouble, and then he locked the door and left."

Jane felt as if she might choke with fear and anger.

"Then what happened," Sarah said, "is that Uncle Billy finally wiggled out of his ropes and he was untying us and that's when Buddy showed up."

"And it's a good thing," Shakura said, "because we were *so* scared!"

"Oh Sarah! Shakura!" Jane said.

"Billy is terribly clever!" Hillary said.

"The man never showed up again?" Beau asked.

Both girls shook their heads.

Beau turned to Buddy. "It's your turn, Buddy. How did you know where to look?"

Buddy shrugged. "It was a little bit of just plain luck, I guess, but I seen when I left here that there had been something parked out front there that was leaking antifreeze. You can smell that stuff, you know. Ain't no mistaking it. So I set out looking for a car that's maybe got a boiling radiator. And like I said, this town ain't that big. I seen this little ol' foreign job. It was parked in front of this place, you know. It was one of them real old houses that are all hooked together kinda like apartments, like the girls said, and so then I went up there and got 'em."

"It was just great when we saw him coming through the window!" Sarah said.

Beau turned his puzzled frown on Buddy. "Through the window? How did you manage to get up there? And what did you do, break the glass?"

"Wasn't no glass. It was boarded up with them, what you call it? Shutters?"

"Then how?"

"I picked up a few tips from them cops when they was investigatin' that break-in back when we first got here, you know."

Beau nodded knowingly. "Oh yeah, the seminar on how to break into a three-hundred-year-old house."

"Something like that." Buddy looked pleased with himself.

"And Billy?" Beau asked.

Buddy shrugged again. "He was madder than hell. Took off to look for that guy. Said he'd be back to the house when he found him."

Both of Hillary's well-manicured hands came up to her face in alarm. "Oh my Lord! That could be dangerous."

Beau stood and looked down at all of them. "You're right about that, Hillary. I'm going after him, and I'll notify Vautrin. The rest of you stay here. Have some dinner. Get a good night's rest." He spoke in his authoritative policeman's voice.

Hillary stood as well. "I'm going with you."

"No. It's best that you stay here." The tone of Beau's voice did not invite argument. Hillary sat down again, slowly. This time it was Jane who reached for Hillary's hand.

15

Sleep pulled at Jane with silken ropes, and the relief she felt at having the girls back allowed her to give in to it. She let it wrap her in its gauzy web until she was deeply nestled in its cocoon.

She heard a sound that seemed to come from a great distance. She ignored it at first but it was persistent, and she opened her eyes, realizing that she was hearing a delicate but continuous tapping at her door.

"Who's there?" Her voice was soft and hoarse as she tried not to awaken the girls sleeping in the next room.

"It's me, lamb."

"Hillary?"

"Are you awake?"

"I am now."

With a resigned sigh, Jane threw the covers off, turned on the light, and padded across the ancient wooden floors to open the door. Buddy, who was in a sleeping bag next to her door, stirred slightly when the light from her room hit his face. He rolled over and mumbled something, and Jane looked into Hillary's troubled face. "What is it now, Hill?"

"I can't sleep."

Jane hesitated a moment, then stepped back, making a sweeping motion with her arm. After what they'd been through together recently, if her friend needed companionship for any reason, she couldn't deny it.

Jane took a moment to reassure herself that the girls were indeed safe in the adjoining room, then closed the door quietly and turned back to Hillary. "I know you're worried about Billy, Hill, and I don't blame you, but—"

Hillary's quick wave created a coral shower of enameled fingertips. "Oh, it's not Billy I'm worried about. He and Beau came home hours ago. He's snoring in our bed."

"Hours ago?" Jane glanced at the clock. It was two A.M. "Did he—"

"Did he find anyone? No. He said he looked all over town and couldn't find the man who kidnapped them, but he was wearing that mask, Billy said, and would have been hard to recognize if he took it off. Then he and Beau ran into Vautrin when he went back to that house where they were held captive. Said he just left it in the policeman's hands. Seems Vautrin was doing some investigating at that house anyway because of that car. You know, the Renault. Seems someone had reported it stolen. It's comforting to know he's on top of it."

"Billy didn't learn anything at all?"

Hillary shook her head. "I don't think so. He was too tired to talk much."

"So . . ."

"So?"

"What are you doing here, Hillary?"

"Well, I couldn't sleep."

"I see." Jane was trying very hard not to become impatient.

Hillary sat down on the bed with a heavy sigh, kicked off her feathery slippers, and leaned against the headboard. "I just can't stop thinking about all that's happened."

"I'd like to forget." Jane took the time to close the door

to the bathroom that connected her room with the girls' room so she and Hillary wouldn't awaken them. "But I can't," she said with her own sigh as she dropped down beside Hillary and stretched her feet out in front of her.

"It all seems so confusing." Hillary put her fingertips delicately to her temples. "It gives me a headache to think about it."

"It's confusing, all right." Jane drew her legs up and crossed them. "And according to Vautrin, nothing is related. By his reckoning, Daudet committed the murders, now he's in jail. The guys who shot at us were just pranksters or drunks, and the kidnapping . . ." Jane glanced at Hillary. "That has to be related. I mean, that note warning us to stop meddling. Stop meddling in what? The murders, of course."

"Do you think Vautrin thinks that's what the notes meant?"

Jane shook her head. "Who knows what Vautrin thinks. It's part of his job to be noncommittal. But he has to see the connection. I mean, how could he help but see it?"

Hillary had taken on a worried look. "If word gets out about all this happening on my tour, I just know I'll be ruined. You've *got* to get this straightened out, Jane, so we can all get on with our lives."

"Excuse me?"

"Just do it. Go talk it over with Vautrin. Beau, too, if that will help. There's still time to salvage this trip and my reputation if you will just do it."

"Hillary . . ."

"Are you going to say I don't pay you enough? Well, let me point out that I pay you more than—"

"It has nothing to do with pay, Hillary. How do you expect me to solve three murders, attempted murder, and kidnapping when the police can't even do it?"

Hillary gave her a perplexed frown. "But you're so clever, Jane. Of course you can do it."

"Not that clever." Jane stood up and opened the bathroom door a crack and listened to make sure she could still hear the girls in the next room, then closed the door again.

"Why are you pacing, Jane?"

"I'm not pacing. I just—"

"Of course you're pacing. You always do that when you're thinking. I just know you're about to come up with something that will solve this."

"Hillary, I told you, I don't know . . ." She stopped, realizing she was pacing. "I'm telling you, I don't know enough to solve this."

"But you must!" Hillary fluffed another pillow and stuck it behind her back. "You just don't know you know it yet."

Jane was still restless. "OK, look, here's all we know." Jane ticked her points off on her fingers. "One, Paul Hayes was strangled and put in a wine vat. Two, Henry McEdwards and a housemaid named Eugenie were found dead in the chapel, also strangled. Three, Guillaume Daudet was arrested for their murders and for having a meth lab in his winery. Four, the police say the three people who died saw the meth lab, and Daudet didn't want them to. Four, before the second murders, someone left cryptic notes in the house warning us that we would be harmed. Five, someone tried to kill us on the autoroute. Six, someone named Louis Gustave tried to kill us at the parade. Seven, someone kidnapped Sarah and Shakura and Billy to scare us off."

Hillary looked up at her expectantly. "Go on."

Jane sat down on the bed, a weary gesture. "What do you mean, go on? That's all there is."

"Why, Jane, honey, you left out the part that you don't think Daudet did it. You left out the question as to why Henry and Eugenie were together. Keep in mind, I have my own theories about that, of course. And you left out the part that those notes were so, well, creepy, with all those Knights Templar implications. You also left out the fact that we think the car the kidnappers were in is the same car that chased us on the autoroute." Hillary shook her head and gave Jane a look that seemed to suggest that Jane was slipping.

Jane straightened her shoulders and leaned toward Hillary, waving a decisive finger. "Nothing you said is fact. You said I don't *feel* Daudet did it, that there's a *question* about Henry and Eugenie, that there were *implications* of things on the creepy notes, that we *think* the cars *may* be the same. It's all just speculation."

"But they're clues, as I said." Hillary sounded more hopeful than confident. "And sometimes your law school education gets in the way of your thinking."

Jane was silent just a few seconds too long.

"Aha! So you agree. There are some clues in all of that."

"I didn't say that."

"But you're thinking it."

"How do you know what I'm thinking?"

Hillary fluttered her fingers in a dismissive wave again. "Oh, I just know, lamb, I just know. We're going to get to the bottom of this."

Jane raised an eyebrow. "Oh, so it's *we* now."

"You need me, Jane. I can see that now. Oh, you're wonderful at logic, but you need someone who's not afraid to try blue and green plaid sofa pillows with pale pink flowered wallpaper."

"What?" Jane felt disoriented, as if she'd missed a part of the conversation.

"In Lottie Wagner's living room, remember? I redid her house for her last fall. There's nothing logical about blue and green plaid with pink flowers."

"I don't think I can disagree with that," Jane said carefully and evenly, not sure where Hillary was going.

"Well, it takes two kind of brains. Your logical one and my, well, creative one."

"Uh-huh."

"Together, we can solve this thing, Jane." Hillary stood and started for the door. "Get some sleep now. We'll get back to this in the morning." She left, giving Jane a cheerful little wave as she walked out the door, apparently willing to relax now that she thought Jane was going to begin an investigation in which she could become involved.

Jane settled into bed again, hoping to sink back into the pleasant numbness she'd been in when Hillary awakened her. Instead, she found herself turning from one side to the next, then onto her stomach, punching her pillow, then staring at the dark shadows on the high ceiling above her.

Maybe Hillary was right. Maybe there were clues right under her nose that she just wasn't seeing. She brushed the thought aside. That was Vautrin's business, not hers. She had enough to do watching out for Sarah and Shakura. She closed her eyes again and willed herself to sleep.

Within a few seconds, her eyelids opened as if they were on springs, and she was staring at the ceiling again and thinking of those notes Hillary had mentioned. Odd that Vautrin hadn't kept them. Seems he should have wanted them for evidence. Hillary had given them to her, and she'd stuck them in a drawer in the old bureau.

She turned on the lamp beside her bed, then got up and went to the bureau. The notes were lying there in the drawer, just where she put them. She picked them up and read the cryptic warnings, stared at the crude lettering done in red ink, fingered the oily edge.

A clue? Not that she could see. She closed the door, got back in bed, and once more tried to go to sleep. This time, it was Henry and Eugenie that kept popping into her mind. Was Hillary right about the reason they'd been together? Was there some clue there?

When she tried to push thoughts of Henry and Eugenie away, they were replaced by two men chasing her and Hillary in a dark Renault. They had worn those silly masks, but there was something about them, something vague, that made her feel she'd seen them before. Why would either of them look familiar? This was a foreign country. She didn't know people here.

Troubling thoughts and questions tumbled in her mind

until almost dawn when she finally fell into an exhausted sleep. She awoke the next morning with a start when she heard Sarah screaming.

A surge of adrenaline propelled her out of bed and across the room. She flung the bathroom door open and rushed through to the adjoining room. Both girls' beds were empty. Something hammered at her chest and in her head, then she heard the scream again and then a giggle, Sarah's giggle, and then Shakura's laughter, followed by a thump.

Jane flung the door to the hallway open, and the two girls faced her, out of breath and ruddy faced from exertion.

Sarah's hand went to her mouth. "Oh, Mom, we woke you up. I'm sorry."

Jane felt disoriented. "What were you doing? What time is it?"

"It's almost ten o'clock. Everybody else has been up for hours," Sarah said. "Mrs. Scarborough said we should let you sleep."

Jane felt even more disoriented. "Ten o'clock? It can't be. Where is—"

"Mrs. Scarborough saved some breakfast for you," Sarah said. "Something weird. I wish we could have pancakes."

"With strawberry syrup like they have at IHOP," Shakura said.

"And a Big Mac for lunch," Sarah added.

Jane left the girls dreaming of the culinary delights of home and went back to her room feeling weak with relief that the girls had simply been playing noisily in the hall. She'd have to get dressed quickly. Hillary would be leaving soon for the morning cooking class, and she'd expect her to be there to take notes.

She'd skip breakfast, she decided, as she pulled on a pair of khaki slacks. Maybe just grab a quick cup of coffee and take only enough time to tell the others good morning and to meet Billy Scarborough.

She brushed her hair quickly and skipped applying any of her makeup except lipstick, then hurried downstairs. She went first to the dining room, where she hoped everyone would still be lingering after breakfast. No one was there, however, except Buddy.

He looked up at her from his breakfast. There was an unexpected guilty expression smeared like egg yolk across his face.

"Miz Ferguson!"

"Good morning, Buddy."

"I hope you won't tell Miz Scarborough about this." He glanced down at his plate.

"About what?"

"Well, I just had to have me some decent breakfast. Ham and eggs. Fixed 'em myself. Wish I could find me some grits, though. Just don't tell Miz Scarborough, OK?"

"Your secret's safe with me, Buddy." Jane glanced around the dining room. "Where's everybody else?"

"Mr. Scarborough and Beau's gone off to talk to that Frenchy policeman, and Miz Scarborough's gone to her school. God, I sure hope it helps her improve. This morning we didn't have nothin' but some kind of fruit thing and cold bread and butter and coffee so strong it near 'bout ate a hole in the cup. She said it was a sentimental breakfast."

"You mean Continental?"

"Whatever. Wasn't worth shit."

"What time did Billy and Beau leave?"

Buddy took another bite of his ham and eggs and washed it down with coffee. "Oh, they ain't been gone long. I woulda gone with them, but somebody had to stay here to see after you and the girls."

"I appreciate that, Buddy." Jane moved toward the door. "I've got to meet Hillary at the school. Promise me you won't let anything happen to Sarah and Sahkura."

"They ain't going to be outta my sight." Buddy stood and followed Jane out of the room to the stairway. As Jane left, he was calling out to the girls, and they answered him with their giggles and squeals.

By the time Jane walked up to the hill to L'École de

Cuisine Hulot, the class was already gathered around the tables, and Madame Hulot was standing at the front of the class, demonstrating how to cook a leg of lamb, which she called *gigot d'agneau*. She had the leg in a large roasting pan, and she was demonstrating how to arrange sprigs of various herbs in the pan.

Jane slid into the seat next to Hillary and whispered, "Why didn't you wake me up?"

"Yesterday was a grueling day, lamb. I thought you needed extra rest."

Jane glanced up at Madame Hulot probing at the mound of raw meat and wished Hillary could refrain from calling her lamb, at least for the moment.

"You missed the *pomme de terre avec gruyère et noix muscade.*"

"Geez."

"Fascinating."

"I'm sure."

Madame Hulot was now going on and on about consommé. Jane was wishing she'd gotten that cup of coffee before she hurried away.

"Make sure you get this down in your notes," Hillary whispered.

"I'll remember." Jane tapped the side of her head with her finger. "It's all up here."

Hillary seemed engrossed in Madame Hulot's lecture, but in a few minutes she leaned toward Jane and whispered again. "Did you meet Billy?"

"He'd gone with Beau to see Vautrin."

"Oh yes, he was going to talk to him about Paul Hayes. Billy said the papers back home are full of the news of his death. He was right important in the banking business, you know."

"I didn't know."

"Well, he was. He was into international banking and all that stuff. That's why he was in France, according to the papers back home. Look at this." She handed Jane a copy of the *Prosper Picayune.* "Billy brought this back with him."

Jane unfolded the paper as quietly as she could and began reading. Indeed, the lead story was all about Paul Hayes. It mentioned his prominence in Alabama, his international banking business, and even the fact that he had once been indicted by a grand jury for bank fraud but that the charges had been dropped.

She leaned toward Hillary and whispered, "He was here on business? I thought he was vacationing. Provence is not exactly the center of international banking. Why was he here and not in Paris? Or London?"

"Or Switzerland, doing something with Swiss bank accounts," Hillary added.

"Switzerland?" Madame Hulot was staring at Jane and Hillary. "A very uninteresting country. Nothing but mountains, and the cuisine is horrible." Once again she'd given the last word the French pronunciation. She glanced at Hillary. "You are not paying attention, Madame Scarborough? You would like to be excused?"

"Why, of course not." Hillary spoke in her best Southern belle voice.

"Ah, well then, let us proceed." Madame Hulot was now mixing bread crumbs with something and talking nonstop about the superiority of the herbs of Provence.

Jane did her best to pay attention, but after the harrowing events of the previous day, leg of lamb and Provençal herbs seemed of little importance. She glanced at the paper again. There was a story about Henry's death, too, and the mention that the funeral was pending the arrival of his wife from France. Reading the stories made her restless for some reason. Her eyes kept wandering to the window. She saw someone, just outside the window, bending and straightening, bending and straightening, turning the soil, obviously, for Madame Hulot's vegetable garden.

When the person straightened his back and turned around slightly as he wiped the sweat from his brow with his forearm, Jane saw that it was Louis. Out of jail so soon? When he had attempted to kill someone? That was both alarming and surprising.

Jane glanced at Hillary, who was deeply absorbed in Madame's demonstration. Jane became aware of the sweet scent of flowers mingling with the smell of fresh lamb.

"The lavender sorbet is simple but *très, très élégant,*" Madame Hulot said as she dropped flower petals into a boiling liquid. "A most distinct taste of Provence," said Madame Hulot, who had by now moved on to dessert.

Jane glanced out the window again and saw a car drive up and park near where Louis was working. She gasped in surprise when she realized that the car was the very same car, the Renault, that had pursued her and Hillary into Monte Carlo. There was smoke coming out of the hood, as if the radiator was boiling, as if it was low on antifreeze. She sat up straighter in her seat and watched as someone got out. Someone she recognized. It was the man whom Hillary had encountered when she was going the wrong way on a narrow one-way street the first day they were in town. She remembered how his anger had turned into admiring and flirty glances at Hillary.

Madame Hulot was now extolling the virtues of lemons, which she called citrons, that grew near the Mediterranean coast in Provence. "The citrons of California are not like these. *Non, non!* They are not so full of the spirit! Ah yes, the soul of the sun and of Provence!"

The driver of the Renault had gotten out of the car and was shouting and waving a threatening fist at Louis, who was also shouting and making menacing gestures with his shovel. The other man turned back to his car, grabbed two things from the front seat, and waved them wildly at Louis, one in each hand. Jane stood up to see better. The man held a wig in one hand, shaggy and long, and in the other was what looked like a child's rubber Halloween mask made to look ugly and frightening.

The wig and mask were the same ones she'd seen on the

man in the parade who was dressed as a Saracen warrior. Could it be the same wig and mask worn by whoever had kidnapped Billy and the girls?

She glanced at Hillary, who was now also staring at the scene outside the window. So was everyone else, she realized. Madame Hulot stopped her lecture and hurried to the window.

"Allez! Allez!" She gestured with her hands as if to shoo them away. *"Vous faites trop de bruit!"* She slammed the window closed and turned back to her class. "Too noisy! What can I do? They are disturbing too much!" She threw up her hands in disgust. "Ah, what can I do? They have disturbed my thoughts. We must take the rest. The break, as you say in America. Yes we must take the break. Go home for lunch. All of you. We will continue this class tomorrow. I cannot think with this noise!"

The members of the class stood and moved toward the door. Hillary stood as well, but she made no move toward the door. "What do you suppose those men were arguing about?" Hillary squinted and leaned closer to the window. "Isn't one of them that awful Louis person who tried to kill us with that pitchfork?"

"Yes, I think so, and the other one is that man you met on the one-way street."

"What man?"

"You know, the one who seemed to like you."

"Oh, well . . ."

"And it was his car that was chasing us on the autoroute near Monte Carlo."

"My lord, Jane, are you sure?"

"Yes. I'm positive. Look at it. Doesn't it look familiar?"

"Well, yes, now that you mention it!"

"And I've been thinking about something. That day we met Lola at the train station . . ."

Hillary raised her eyebrows in curiosity. "What about it?"

"I'm not sure I have it all put together yet, but I think I

know who killed Paul and Henry and Eugenie."

Hillary grabbed Jane's hands. "Jane! I knew you could do it. Who?"

"Well, I'm not sure, but I think it was—"

"I am so sorry that this has happened. I am sure it is very, um, unsetting." Sparks of energy seemed to emanate from Madame Hulot as she moved toward them, talking with her hands as well as her voice.

"You mean upsetting," Hillary said.

"Yes, upsettling!" Madame Hulot's arms were mobile punctuation marks. "Men! They are such children. Always argue! One is saying, 'You steal my car. You leave your dirty costume in my car. I will have you in jail.' And the other, that lazy no-good Louis, says, 'Jail! Ha! I work for the police!' He is crazy!" Madame Hulot touched her head with a fingertip. "That Louis is crazy. He works for the police? No, the police think he is crazy, too. Even Vautrin, who has no taste—I suppose he cannot be blamed that he is Swiss and not French, but you should see the way he eats—even Vautrin thinks the idiot Louis is crazy. Vautrin comes to me and says Louis will work for me for one week for no pay. That is his punishment, he says. Because he is too crazy to stay in jail, he says. And now do you hear what that crazy, no-good Louis says? That he is a spy for the government. He is *touché.*" She pointed to her head again.

"But you agreed to take Louis on? To let him work for you?" Jane asked.

"But of course. It is, as you say, good deal, because I do not have to pay. It is the public service as the punishment."

Jane frowned, thinking, trying to make sense of it. "But why you?"

Madame Hulot took on the look of a bird with puffed feathers. "Why me? Why, Vautrin and the judge who sentenced Louis admire my school, of course. L'École de Cuisine Hulot is important to the village of Lenoir. Bringing in tourist who spend money, you know. Ah yes, even the mayor would say L'École de Cuisine Hulot is important to Lenoir."

Hillary nudged Jane. "I am just dying for you to tell me who—"

"Ask anyone," Madame Hulot said. "Even those who don't come to the school for my wonderful classes will come to admire it. Even Monsieur and Madame Mc-Edwards, who come with you to stay in the château. Were they not here on the day the poor man died? Standing just outside my door. They were here to see my school, I am sure. Ah, but the argument," she waved her hands again.

"Henry and Lola were arguing?" Hillary asked. "Oh my!" She glanced at Jane.

"Oh no," Madame Hulot waved her hand in a gesture of dismissal. "Not with each other, with Monsieur Vautrin."

"What were they arguing about?" Jane could almost feel Hillary's growing excitement.

"Money, of course. What else?"

"Money? Why would Henry and Lola argue with a complete stranger about money?" Hillary glanced from Madame Hulot to Jane, wearing a puzzled frown.

"Oh, it was something about the death of the other poor American. His money, I think. You all know each other, don't you. You will understand better than I." She glanced out the window and frowned. "That lazy man is leaving! Look at him! He walks away leaving my work unfinished. He thinks he can cheat me? Ha! I will show him!" She bustled away, leaving through the back door.

Jane thought for a moment about what Madame Hulot had just said. "Oh my God!" she said when she realized the implications of it. She grabbed Hillary's hand and pulled her toward the door. "We've got to go get Beau and Billy."

"Now?" Hillary pulled back, reluctant to leave. "Why do we have to go get them now?"

"Because if we don't, Vautrin may kill them the way he did Paul and Henry and Eugenie."

"I'm afraid you're too late." Vautrin came through the front door, his police revolver drawn and pointed at Jane and Hillary. "And now it is your turn," he said as he raised the pistol to Jane's head.

16

"Mister Vautrin? What on earth are you thinking about, pointing a gun at us like that?" Realization seemed to come slowly to Hillary. She sucked in her breath and glanced at Jane. "Oh my Lord, Jane, you did figure it out! But how—"

Jane was staring at the end of the gun barrel, which was still leveled at her head, and found it impossible to reply.

"And what have you done with Billy and Beau?" Hillary insisted.

"Shut up!" Vautrin said. He moved the gun and pointed it at Hillary's head.

"Some people here in this country are just so rude!" Hillary looked as if she might be about to cry. "And it's really not necessary, you know. *Shut up* is just not a phrase that we use in the best circles where I come from. I think you should—"

"Hillary!" Jane spoke quietly but firmly between teeth clenched tight with fear.

"What?"

"Shut . . . I mean, be quiet, for Christ's sake." Jane's eyes were still on the gun.

"Well, I would just like to know how you knew—"

"And so would I like to know," Vautrin said. "I think you see too much, know too much. That is not good for you, to know too much, you know. I try to frighten you away, but you are very, um stubborn?"

Jane was suddenly filled with anger. "It was you in the car chasing us on the autoroute, wasn't it? And you tried to kill us in the casino. You and that deputy. You were wearing those dumb masks. And you're the bastards who kidnapped my daughter and her friend." Jane's anger unleashed everything she'd been thinking.

Hillary turned to her, surprised. "How did you know that, Jane?"

Jane didn't answer until Vautrin barked, "Tell her!" He waved the gun at her.

"The brown suit and gray tie!" Jane's voice squeaked with fear. She didn't take her eyes off the gun.

"What?" Hillary asked.

"Remember? Vautrin told us his deputy was color-blind? I remembered what you said about the way he was dressed, a brown suit and gray tie. That was when I first started to suspect something."

Vautrin chuckled, still holding the gun pointed at her head. "You are indeed far too clever." He moved the gun closer. "I will take no pleasure in killing one as clever as you, but," he shrugged again, *"c'est nécessaire."* He cocked his head and smiled at Jane. "I am sure you understand why."

Jane could only manage to shake her head.

"You are very amusing." Vautrin gave her what, under different circumstances, might have been a charming smile. "Why don't you tell me more about what you know? Perhaps your detective skills will come in handy for me someday."

Jane shook her head again.

Vautrin took a quick step closer and placed the gun barrel directly against her head. Hillary drew a sharp breath, and Jane could see her frightened eyes.

"You will tell me exactly how you came to know what you know. It is surprising to me that an American woman would be so good at this." Vautrin's face was very close to Jane, and he had definitely lost his charming look. Jane could feel the gun barrel against her head.

"Those notes!" Jane said quickly, fear making her voice tremble. "The oily film on that paper. Then I saw that deputy of yours spraying wax on the paper cutter. It made me start wondering, and I thought the notes must have come from your office."

"Ah!" Vautrin nodded his head. "But that could not have been enough." Vautrin moved away from Jane again, but he still had the gun trained on her.

Jane didn't take her eyes off the gun. "It was that man whose car you borrowed who gave it away. He accused Louis of stealing his car and of leaving those masks and costumes inside, and Louis kept insisting he worked for the police. You must have convinced that man that it was Louis who stole his car just because he was retarded and didn't know what he was doing. You tried the same thing with us, telling us he didn't know what he was doing when he threatened us, but you must have hired the poor fool to kill us."

Vautrin shook his head. "You are, how do you say? Jumping conclusions? You could not possibly prove anything. You will tell me more," he said with a menacing wave of the gun.

"I . . . I heard Louis say he was working for the police," Jane said, "and I heard the owner of the car—that Renault you were in when you were chasing us—complain that Louis stole it, and he found those masks in the car. I just had a hunch you hired Louis because you failed to get us in Monte Carlo."

"You had a what?" Vautrin looked confused.

"A hunch. A guess, that's all. I didn't know anything for sure."

"Ah, then it was Maurice again. My deputy is an idiot! First he gives it away with his unmatched clothes, then his wax can, and then mask and wig he leaves in the car." Vautrin took on a resigned smile. "Ah well, it's just as well that he will be dead, as soon as I finish my use of him. I did not really want to pay him what I offered him anyway."

"Dead?" Hillary croaked.

Vautrin ignored her. He was still looking at Jane. "There is more. I know there is more."

"It was Daudet." Jane's voice trembled with the fear that he might kill both her and Hillary if she didn't cooperate. "I knew that he couldn't possibly have killed Henry and Eugenie because, in spite of what you said, he had already been arrested when they died. I guessed that Henry must have learned something the killer didn't want him to know. And the story about the meth lab. It had to be false, just a way to implicate Daudet. I knew that because Beau and I were all over that winery and we would have seen it if it was there."

"That's right," Hillary said. "So if Daudet was arrested on trumped-up charges, then the police had to be involved." She turned to Jane. "You are just so smart, lamb."

Vautrin frowned. "I do not understand this 'trumped up,' but you are right; planting the lab and paying the employee to testify against Daudet was a simple matter. I already had the lab that I had confiscated during another arrest. But I think Jane is not as smart as you say if she is keeping something from me. She has not told me everything."

"I don't know everything!" Jane's words came in quick, nervous bursts. "I don't know why you were using all those symbols of the Knights Templar, and I'm not sure why you had to kill poor Eugenie."

Vautrin laughed again, a soft chuckle that, under different circumstances, would have been benign but that sounded maniacal to Jane now. "You yourself gave me the idea for the Knights Templar when I see you are so interested in the ancient legends. You see, I am a member of *les Macons* and of the order of Knights Templar. Fitting, as you say, because the Templars were bankers, just like poor Paul. It was a nice touch, those symbols, *n'est-ce pas?* And Eugenie? Ah yes, poor Eugenie indeed. She was too eager to work for me to have the charges dropped for selling the drugs. She was only to place the notes where I tell her, but she is too curious. She learns too much, just as you have, so I had to kill her, just as I must kill you."

"Well, I just don't understand why you have to kill so many people from Prosper." Hillary sounded exasperated. "It is a real nice town. If you ever visit there, you'll see what I mean."

Jane turned to Hillary in disbelief. "For Christ's sake, Hillary, are you inviting him?"

"Well . . ."

"Perhaps I will visit someday." Vautrin sounded perfectly charming. "I have a fondness for the American South."

"Oh yeah," Jane said, in spite of herself. "You said you've been to Atlanta, and you know Jim Ed. That must have been where you met Paul Hayes."

"You are correct." Vautrin took a step forward, bringing the gun barrel close to Jane's head again. "But that means nothing. Unless you have hunched more." He jabbed the gun into her temple. "What else have you hunched?"

Jane swallowed hard to keep her voice from trembling. It did little good. "Hayes came close to being indicted for embezzlement once, but he got off. The newspaper said it was thought he was putting the money in a Swiss bank account, but it could never be proven. You were involved somehow. Maybe helped him set it up, since you're Swiss and not French. But he must have been trying to cheat you, so you killed him."

Vautrin frowned and brought his other hand up to steady the gun. *"Mon dieu!* You are very good at this hunching."

There was another audible intake of breath from Hillary as realization came to her. "And Henry! He's an accountant and an auditor for the bank. He must have been the one who found out about it, so you killed him."

"Hillary!" Jane tried to give her a warning glance, but she was afraid to move her head. "Don't . . ."

Jane heard a click as Vautrin cocked the gun. "Enough!" he said. "I have heard enough."

Jane could see, from the corner of her eye, his finger twitch slightly as he prepared to tighten it on the trigger. Then suddenly, Madame Hulot appeared in the doorway. In one quick moment she took in what was happening and grabbed the leg of lamb from the table next to the door. She swung it like a club and hit Vautrin's head from behind. He fell, and his gun landed with a thud at Jane's feet. The gun discharged, sending a bullet through the leg of lamb. All three women screamed, and Jane tried to grab the gun, but she was not quick enough. Vautrin's hand reached it before hers did. He raised it to fire, but in the same moment, Hillary threw something in his eyes.

"Take that, you damn Yankee!" Hillary's voice was shrill. "It's the sun and soul of Provence."

Vautrin cried out in agony, and the gun fell to the floor, once again causing it to discharge, but this time there were no screams.

"Citron!" Madam Hulot said, laughing and patting Hillary on the back. *"Très bien!"*

Suddenly, the door opened again and both Louis and the man who had accused him of stealing his car barged into the building, both of them all shoulders and arms logjamming the doorway.

"Qui est atteint?" Louis said, his gaze darting around the room.

"Quelqu'un est blessé? Nous avons entendu un coup de feu!" the other man said, and then, *"Mon dieu!"* when he saw Vautrin on the floor, his hands covering his face as he writhed in pain.

Madame Hulot began one of her rapid onslaughts of French as she waved her arms and backed the men away from Vautrin. Jane was trying, in spite of her shaking, to keep the gun trained on him.

Both men spewed animated phrases back at Madame Hulot in an incomprehensible exchange that made Jane even more nervous. Madame Hulot glanced at her and must have seen how unsteady she looked.

"It is nothing," she said. "They hear the gunshot and come in to see what is wrong. Louis is now saying he never worked for Vautrin, but he is lying, of course. He is the idiot." She pointed to her own head and shook it as if to demonstrate Louis's lack of brains. "And François . . ." Madame Hulot's eye brows arched twice in rapid succession. "He says Madame Scarborough is the most beautiful woman he has ever seen and he wants to assure himself that she is not harmed."

"Well, we don't have time for him to do an examination." Jane's voice, like her body, was trembling. "We've go to do something with Vautrin before Lola shows up."

"Lola?" Hillary wore a puzzled look. "Why, she's back home in Prosper by now." Hillary glanced nervously at François.

Jane shook her head. "I don't think so. The newspaper Billy brought with him said Henry's funeral was pending until Lola could return from France."

Hillary frowned. "Why would she still be here? She was going to leave as soon as the body was released, and Vautrin said it would be released within a day."

"She never intended to go back, and she was never in Avignon, either, was she, Vautrin?" Jane said. "That arrival at the train station must have been staged by the two of you."

Vautrin, still on the floor, made a move as if to get to his feet, but Jane thrust the gun forward. "Stay where you are!" Jane glanced around the room. "You! François! Go notify the police in one of these neighboring villages. Tarascon maybe. Or Beaucaire."

Madame Hulot translated Jane's command, and François hurried away with Louis in tow.

"Now!" Jane said, still fighting to keep from trembling. "Tell me what you've done with Beau Jackson and Billy Scarborough."

"They are safe! They are safe!" Vautrin, still on the floor, tried to scramble away when Jane jabbed the gun at him. "Maurice is holding them. He will do nothing until I come back to tell him to kill them."

"Well, my Lord!" It was hard to tell whether Hillary's exclamation was fear or relief. She turned toward Jane again. "But what's this you're saying about Lola? You think she's still here?"

"Yes." Jane was still keeping a close watch on Vautrin. "I think she was mixed up in this embezzlement business somehow. That must have been what they were arguing about with Vautrin. And since you haven't killed her yet," she said to Vautrin, "that must mean she knew about and condoned both Paul's and Henry's deaths."

Vautrin looked up at Jane with his acid-reddened eyes. A sound escaped his throat that might have been meant to be a laugh, but it came out more as an agonizing groan. "Condone? You are saying, I think, that she agreed? Ha! It is more than that. She is the murderer in all three cases. I am innocent. I have no blood on my hands. It is that woman! She strangled all three of them, and then she convinces me to put the blame on Daudet. She was sure you saw us that night at the winery, and she tried to trick you into thinking she was only jogging. I had to hurry away on my bicycle."

"Lola?" Hillary was momentarily aghast. Then she turned to Jane. "Didn't I tell you she killed Henry? Didn't I tell you from the very beginning?"

"You did, Hill, but I think you got the motive wrong. It wasn't because she found Henry cheating on her with Eugenie. It must have been something else. Greed?"

Vautrin nodded, eager to clear himself by implicating Lola. "Greed. Yes, of course, greed. And revenge. Monsieur Hayes was cheating. Keeping more than his share, so Lola killed him. 'Now we will have his share, too,' she said. And Henry? But, of course he knew. He even helped her lure Monsieur Hayes into the winery. That is where you almost caught them." Vautrin put a hand to his burning eyes. "We would have had no problem except Madame Lola becomes even more the greedy one. If Henry is dead, then she will have more, she says. So she kills the husband."

"You bastard! I should have killed you long ago!" It was Lola who was standing in the doorway this time. She was dressed in a neon green jumpsuit with too much jewelry, and she held a gun. She glanced at Jane. "Put that gun on the floor, Janey, baby, easy now."

Jane put the gun on the floor, and Vautrin scrambled to retrieve it. As soon as he had his hand on it, Lola fired, wounding him in the shoulder. Lola kicked the gun out of the way. She glanced at the blood seeping through Vautrin's fingers where he held his shoulder.

Lola sneered at him. "I was aiming for your heart, you shithead Frog. I won't miss next time, if I don't decide to let you bleed to death first." She fired the gun again, this time hitting him in the foot. "Blame it all on me, will you?" she said, as Vautrin crumpled and cried out in agony. "I couldn't have gotten that creep Hayes in the wine vat without you, and I couldn't have gotten Henry and that stupid bitch up on on that altar, either, but that doesn't make you worthy of my little finger, much less a share of the profit." She glanced around the room. "It's a good thing I got here when I did. I had a feeling you were going to mess things up. It's been nothing but one foul-up after another. First these two spot Henry handing Paul that information on the new Swiss account when we were in the airport, and now you! I told you we needed to get rid of these two long ago. Now I've got to get rid of you, too."

"Lola, please . . ."

Lola ignored Vautrin's anguish and waved the gun at Hillary, Jane, and Madame Hulot. "Against the wall, all of you, while I decide how I'm going to get rid of you."

The three women walked backward toward the wall, afraid to take their eyes off of Lola and the gun. Then, suddenly, Hillary stumbled and fell to the floor.

"Hillary!" Jane cried.

"Madame!" Madame Hulot said.

"What are you doing, you clumsy fool?" Lola's voice was edged with panic as she turned her attention to Hillary.

In one quick movement, Hillary straightened herself to a sitting position and pointed Vautrin's gun at Lola. Jane realized Hillary had covered the gun with her body as she fell, and she realized, too, that the whole thing had been deliberate.

"Now both of y'all just stay where you are, do you hear me?" Hillary held the gun with both hands as she pointed it at Vautrin and Lola. "You had better put that gun down, Lola McEdwards. I just want you to know you have a foul mouth and you don't have any taste at all when it comes to clothes."

"Hillary!" Jane screamed, when she saw that Lola, who had at first been stunned by Hillary's move, had now come to her senses and had cocked the gun.

Then, suddenly, a shot rang out. Jane felt her heart drop to her stomach, and she knew a moment of blinding fear until she realized that it had been Hillary's gun that had fired, and that Lola's hand was bleeding and her gun was on the floor. Jane came to her senses enough to reach for it.

"*Très bien! Très bien!*" Madame Hulot jumped up and down with excitement.

Hillary got to her feet, and she and Jane both kept their guns trained on the prisoners.

"That was great, Hill. You were wonderful!" Jane's breath was coming in short gasps.

"I was aiming for her heart," Hillary said.

It seemed an eternity when, in reality, it was only a few minutes before Jane heard the sound of a car approaching. Madame Hulot had been talking, first in French and then in English. "Ah, François has brought the police! *Mais oui!* He is very dependable, that François. Not like Louis. He is an idiot and he is lazy, that Louis! 'He will work for you,' Vautrin says to me. 'That is the punishment we give him,' he says. Ha! What work, Vautrin? I should have known you were the idiot as well. You are Swiss! Of course! What can one expect?"

She was still talking when Beau walked in the door.

"Beau!" Jane gasped. "What are you doing here? I mean, how did you—"

"It wasn't hard to get the drop on that deputy, and I got here as fast as I—"

"Where's Billy?" Hillary asked.

Beau took in the scene, including the blood flowing from the various wounds Lola and Vautrin had sustained. "My God! What happened here?"

At that same moment, Jane heard the sound of a siren. She still held the gun trained on Vautrin.

"That must be the police Billy notified," Beau said.

Madam Hulot shook her head. "No, no, it was François who notified—"

"Where did you say Billy is?" Hillary asked, also still keeping her gun on Lola.

"Who's François?" Beau asked.

"C'est moi," François said as he and Louis stepped in the door, accompanied by the police from Beaucaire. François glanced at Hillary. "Madame! *Tu es blessé?"* He took the gun from Hillary and led her toward a chair, making gentle cooing noises.

"Thank God Billy called the police," Beau said, ignoring both Hillary and François, as he took the gun from Jane.

He was eyeing the three policemen who were busy clamping handcuffs on their prisoners.

"No, no, it was François who called the police," Madame Hulot said.

"Who's François?" Beau said.

"Where's Billy?" Hillary asked, refusing a glass of wine François had fetched for her from Madame Hulot's kitchen.

"I was going to tell you," Beau said. "Billy had a call from the U.S. attorney in Alabama. They want him to testify for the prosecution about Lola's role in the embezzlement scheme. Seems she's been under investigation for a long time. Billy was the first one to tip them off that something was going on. He was in a position to do that, since he has a lot of dealings with the bank. He knew something was wrong. He just didn't know who was involved."

"Oh, yes, Billy is so clever!" Some of the color had come back to Hillary's face. "But where *is* he?"

"You're not going to believe this," Beau said, "but the DA said it was urgent. Billy's on his way to Prosper right now."

EPILOGUE

When the doorbell rang at Jane's front door, she checked her hair and makeup quickly in the hall mirror. She was going to have to do something about that makeup. Learn to apply it more artfully maybe, because she could still see the circles under her eyes—evidence that she was still a bit jet lagged.

No time to worry about that now, though. *What you see is what you get,* she thought as she opened the door. Beau was standing there with a bouquet of the prize-winning roses he'd picked from his own garden in one hand and a bottle champagne in the other. He smiled broadly when he saw her, and his eyes swept the length of her. He greeted her with a single word.

"Wow!"

She was wearing a short, sleeveless shift made of black silk she'd bought at the street market in Lenoir just before they'd left.

Jane blushed. "Well, thank you. Oh, and thank you for the roses, too," she said, taking them from him. "I'll just put them in some water."

"It's good to be back, isn't it?" Jane called from the kitchen where she'd gone to get a vase.

"Sure is." Beau had joined her in the kitchen and was leaning against the door frame, the champagne bottle still in his hand.

"You know, I was wondering," Jane said, filling the vase with water, "just how did Billy notify the police in France without an interpreter?"

"Oh he had an interpreter," Beau said.

"Really? Who?"

"Remember that policeman in Monte Carlo you talked to when you were released from jail?"

"How could I forget?"

"Well, he knew that Vautrin as well as Lola and Henry were under suspicion for embezzlement and that Swiss bank account scheme. After he talked to the two of you, he was able to put it all together."

"But where does Billy come into this?"

"Billy Scarborough goes to Monte Carlo on business frequently, you know, and it turns out he knew this cop. He called him after he and I managed to get away from that deputy in Lenoir. The Monte Carlo cop speaks pretty good English, as you probably remember, so he called the police in Beaucaire for us."

Jane put the flowers in the center of the kitchen table and gave them an admiring look. "So was it really Billy or was it François who got the cops there?"

"Does it matter?" Beau reached for her hand and pulled her toward him. "I don't want to talk about Billy or François right now. Not when I'm with a beautiful woman." He had pulled her very close. She could smell the Old Spice. She could feel, ever so slightly, the brush of his lips against hers as he spoke again, his voice soft and husky. "All that time in France and I never got you alone, but now . . ."

Jane felt dizzy. She had to close her eyes. But they flew open suddenly when the telephone rang. Her first thought was to let it ring, but Sarah was at Shakura's house for a sleep over. What if something had happened to her?

"I—I've got to get that." She pulled away reluctantly and picked up the receiver to the kitchen phone.

"Hello," she said, vaguely aware her voice was sultry, deeper than it usually sounded.

"Jane, lamb! Are you all right?"

"Hillary!" Jane glanced at Beau. "Yes, yes, I'm fine."

"Your voice sounds funny."

"I'm fine, Hillary."

"I'm worried about you, Jane. All that murder business while we were gone. It was hard on all of us."

"Yes, yes it was, but I think I'll be all right."

Beau popped the cork on the champagne. "What was that noise?" Hillary asked.

"What noise?"

"Must be something wrong with this connection we have. I'll speak louder."

Jane watched Beau pour the champagne in glasses he pulled from her cupboard. He walked toward her with both glasses in his hand.

"I was thinking about that leg of lamb," Hillary said.

Beau had put the glasses on the table and reached for Jane.

"Oooh," Jane said.

"Yes, it was good wasn't it? But I was thinking I might substitute potatoes for the bread crumbs, and . . ."

"Mmmm, don't stop," Jane said.

"Well, I never knew you liked potatoes that well, Jane. Anyway, I was thinking I would feature the lamb on my next show, and there are some things I want you to get for me so I'll have them in the studio when I . . . Jane, I swear I hear heavy breathing on this line. It *must* be a bad connection."

MADAME HULOT'S LEG OF LAMB

4   cloves garlic, peeled and chopped
4   tablespoons olive oil
1   leg of lamb, approximately 5 pounds
½   teaspoon salt
¼   teaspoon pepper
4   springs rosemary
3   sprigs thyme
3   bay leaves
1   cup bread crumbs
¼   cup chopped scallions
⅓   cup consommé

Combine garlic and olive oil and rub the meat with the mixture. Salt and pepper meat. Place herbs around the lamb. Roast at 400 degrees for about 40 minutes. Mix bread crumbs and scallions and add mixture to pan. Continue roasting about 10 minutes or until thermometer registers desired degree of doneness. Remove lamb and bread crumb mixture from pan and cut into thin slices. Bring consommé to boil in pan in which you have cooked the lamb. Reduce heat and simmer for 5 minutes, scraping bottom of pan to release drippings. Pour over lamb and bread crumb mixture.

You may substitute potatoes for the bread crumbs. Cut them into ¼-inch rounds and boil for about 8 minutes with thinly sliced onions, then place in bottom of roasting pan with lamb on top. Roast approximately one hour or until thermometer registers desired degree of doneness.